BITTER AUTUMN

Book 2 of Northern Intrigue Series

LYN COTE

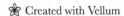 Created with Vellum

Dedication

For You, O God, have proved us; You have tried us, as silver is tried.

—*Psalms* 66:10

For grace are ye saved through faith, not works, lest any man should boast.

—*Ephesians* 2:8–9

This book is dedicated to everyone who's suffered because of someone else's gossip and/or lies.

Chapter 1

Deputy Sheriff Trish Franklin wished she could be a thousand miles away; in fact, anywhere but Winfield, Wisconsin. Still in her uniform, she drove the sheriff's Jeep down the familiar wooded road. Dread sat in her midsection as solid as a brick. The tears she'd held back for two September days—ever since Sheriff Harding had shown her the bad-news letter—suddenly poured down her face. Blinded, she pulled off the road onto the entrance to a grassy private road. She bent her forehead to the padded steering wheel. How could God let this happen?

GREY LAWSON STARED out the bus window. The farther north he rode, the more he noted early-autumn golds and reds in the late-afternoon light painting the trees passing by the window. Grey wished he could stop the bus and just start walking anywhere—anywhere but where he had to go. Behind him on the crowded bus, a baby cried, sounding frustrated and pushed past its limits. Grey understood the mood. *But I have no choice. She needs me. I owe her. I love her.*

An old guy sat crumpled up beside him, a man who'd grown old behind bars. They'd gotten on the bus together, sat together. But they hadn't exchanged a look or a word in hours. Now nearing nightfall, the bus slowed. "Ashford!" the driver announced.

The old man beside Grey finally stirred. The bus stopped and he unfolded himself from his seat. Standing, he cast a departing glance toward Grey. "Good luck," he mumbled. Grey nodded. He watched the old guy shuffle to the front and lower himself step-by-step to the street on the obviously poor side of town.

The bus finished letting off the few other people for this stop and then started up again. The bus driver announced, "Next stop, Winfield!" Grey tried not to look back but couldn't help himself. The old guy stood, clutching his suitcase, looking around. No one was there to meet him. *Good luck, old man.* Grey closed his eyes and prayed that the old guy would find a warm bed and a friendly smile before nightfall.

———

FINALLY, TRISH QUIETED and leaned back against the headrest. Tears still dripped from her chin. She drew in the fresh pine-scented air through the open window. *If I'd suspected this was going to happen, Lord, I'd have stayed in Madison.* Guilt, instant and fierce, scored her like a sharp stinging claw.

No time for regrets. She had to face reality. And reality was Grey Lawson was coming back to town—and it was facing her father and telling him this hard truth. He had to be told today. But she didn't have to face her father alone. Three of her brothers would be with her. She started the engine and pulled back onto the quiet county road. She glanced at her watch. She was already late. Her brothers should be at her father's place by now.

GREY RECOGNIZED THE scenery on the highway into Winfield as if he'd seen it recently, instead of seven years ago. He stood and walked, swaying with the bus's motion toward the driver. He gripped the cool metal rail beside the driver and asked, "Can you let me off at the next intersection? It's closer to home and I'm walking the rest of the way."

The driver glanced at him sideways. "You don't have luggage stowed underneath, do you?"

"No, just this." Grey waved his slack duffel.

"Sure. No problem."

Grey remained where he was, swaying and bobbing with the bus's movement. The intersection of Cross-cut Road and the highway loomed ahead. The bus slowed; Grey moved down the metal stair and waited for the door to part. As soon as it did, he stepped out. He paused while the bus door closed and the long vehicle pulled away. Then he tugged up the hood of his gray sweatshirt and started down Cross-cut, heading toward home. He had a warm bed and a welcoming smile waiting for him. But from just one person, and his arrival might cause her harm. *How can I prevent my return from hurting her?*

TRISH TURNED WEST ONTO CROSS-CUT. Mist was beginning to form in the low spots—cool autumn air brushing against still-warm earth. She sharpened her watchfulness. Twilight was the most dangerous time to drive through the forest. She kept a watch out for the reflection of her headlights onto deer eyes, sometimes the only way to see them in time. A man in a gray hooded sweatshirt was walking west, his back to her. The man turned and lifted a hand with his thumb out.

Hitchhiking was illegal. Trish nearly passed him by but it

was best to let a transient know that the Winfield Sheriff's Department was vigilant. Normally she'd have been driving her own red SUV home, but it was in the garage till tomorrow. So she slowed and pulled off to where he'd paused.

Trish got out and motioned him to come to her. He stared at her and didn't move. "Over here," she ordered in her cop voice.

With halting steps, the stranger approached her. The hood shadowed his face. Was he a wanted man? She rested her hand on her sidearm and took up the defensive stance that had become second nature to her.

The man halted a few paces in front of her.

"Do you have ID?" she asked.

He nodded.

"May I see it?"

He reached into his back jeans pocket and pulled out a battered wallet. He handed it to her.

She opened it and stared down at the faded photograph and the name, Grey Lawson. Her hand trembled as she stared at the photo. This is creepy. *Why would I have to be the one to drive past Grey Lawson here tonight?*

The dread that had started her hands shaking, quivered inch by inch through her whole body. Finally one-handed, she flapped the wallet closed and handed it to him. Did he see her shivering? "Where you headed?" she asked in a gruff voice that didn't even sound like hers.

"My aunt's house. Elsie Ryerson."

She'd known this would be his answer. A feud seethed in Trish's breast. This was the man who was going to make her life hell for the foreseeable future. Yet he was Elsie's nephew and Elsie was at home, probably watching anxiously out the window for him. Trish swallowed down a pulsing knot of bitter words. "Get in. I'll drive you there."

"I can walk—"

"Get in," she ordered, hustling back behind the wheel, her eyes avoiding his. *Let's just get this over. Lord, I wouldn't do this for anyone but Elsie.*

Grey ambled over, let himself in and then settled gingerly onto the passenger seat as if it were spiked with tacks.

Without a word, Trish pulled back onto the road. Her face burned upward from her neck to her roots. Dear God, don't let anyone see me driving with Grey Lawson in my car. My father will explode if he finds out.

As she drove west on Cross-cut, the mist wisped upward on both sides of the road. The dark evergreen forest crowded close on both shoulders of the road. Grey Lawson's presence unfurled in the oppressive silence wedged between them. She could smell his soap and hear him draw breath. The narrow road began to wind near a small lake. The silence pressed down on her lungs, making it hard for her to breathe.

And then she heard squealing tires. The crunch of an impact. A loud one.

She eased off the gas pedal, slowing around a blind curve. Her neck tightened with apprehension about what she'd find. Ahead on the road, her lights highlighted the accident. The nose of a blue pickup truck was perched into the soft shoulder. A large deer covered its front windshield. Trish snapped on her radio and called the accident in to dispatch.

"Anyone hurt?" the dispatcher asked.

"I'll let you know." Trish switched off the radio as she parked beside the accident. Her blue lights rotated, warning any oncoming vehicles. But the road was deserted. She got out and suddenly, she recognized the truck. She sprinted toward the vehicle. "Andy!" she shouted. "Andy!"

She wrenched open the driver's side door and gasped. Her eldest brother was pinned to his seat by the deer's head which had come through the windshield. Blood from the deer or Andrew, or both, smeared the window and dash.

"It's Andy Franklin," Grey said right behind her.

"My brother," she blurted out.

"Is he breathing?"

Grey's no-nonsense words snapped her back to routine. She pressed two fingers to Andy's neck, feeling for the carotid pulse. She found it. "He's breathing and his heart's beating."

"That antler looks like trouble."

Trish followed Grey's hand motion and saw that it was true. One of the antlers was piercing Andy's chest dangerously near the heart. She pulled out her cell phone. Before she could speed dial, the truck shifted and the antler came out of her brother's chest. A tiny thread of blood spurted and pulsed again and again.

Grey shouldered her out of the way. He pressed his large hand down over the wound. "I bet it's nicked an artery. Here." He began shrugging a shoulder out of his sweatshirt. "Take this off me. We can use it for a pressure bandage."

Trish didn't waste any time disputing. She helped Grey out of his sweatshirt. She tugged the sleeve over his hand that pressed down on the wound. When he signaled with a nod, she yanked it over and off the rest of the way. His hand immediately returned to her brother's chest. Deftly she folded the main part of the shirt into a large pad. She put it right next to Grey's hand, right next to the widening, frightening scarlet stain on Andy's shirt. At Grey's nod, she slid it under his barely raised hand and then his hand came down, staunching the blood flow.

"I don't think we should wait for the ambulance," he said. "Even with me exerting pressure, he's losing a lot of blood. I'll get in the back of your Jeep and with your siren blaring, you can drive us to the hospital faster."

Trish hesitated only a moment. "Right." Any delay could cost her brother his life. "Can you carry him?"

"No problem."

"Ease him out. While you carry him, I'll apply the pressure."

"Right."

The two of them maneuvered Andy to the edge of the truck's front seat. At the last moment, Grey let her get into position so she could press down on his chest wound while Grey carried Andy to her Jeep.

"Now!" Grey commanded her. They changed places. Then she was pressing down hard and jogging to keep up with Grey as he hurried to her back door. Warm blood wet her fingers. Grey managed to back into the rear seat with Andy's upper body in his arms. "Okay!" Grey hoisted Andy all the way in and then pressed down on the bloody shirt. "Drive!"

She leaped into the driver's seat and switched on her siren. A quick U-turn and she was barreling down the road, back to the highway toward Ashford. She smelled her brother's blood from her hands that now slipped on the steering wheel. But she didn't look down or pause to clean them. Her eyes on the road, she couldn't afford to hit another deer or a heedless driver. "Is he all right?"

"The same. Just get us there. *Fast.*"

The fog was rolling over the highway as she raced south and then east. She radioed dispatch to alert the hospital. And then she pressed down harder on the gas pedal. She ignored the speedometer. And she prayed, "God, get us there in time. We can't lose Andy, too. Please. Help."

"Yes, Father, please," Grey agreed from behind her.

She hadn't realized that she'd spoken aloud.

But Grey took up the prayer and began reciting what she recognized as one of the Psalms—the Twenty-Third Psalm. The words, "valley of the shadow of death," strangled her. She pressed down harder on the gas pedal. Someday Andrew would dwell in the house of the Lord forever. But she didn't want it to be today.

Finally, the lights of the hospital in Ashford glowed through the mist. She screeched to a halt in front of the Emergency entrance. Hospital staff streamed out of the automatic doors. Within minutes, Andrew was inside, with doctors and nurses swarming around him.

Trish stood outside the treatment area, feeling as if the top of her head wanted to lift off. Or conversely, everything inside her might drain out through her toes. A crazy muddle of sensations and emotions.

"You need to sit down."

She glanced up at Grey who stood looking down at her. "I..."

He pulled her by the arm to a blue molded fiberglass chair. "Sit."

She sank down, waves of nausea pounding her. She usually didn't react like this to blood, to accidents. *But this is Andy.*

A receptionist came over with a clipboard. "Do you know the patient's name?"

"Andrew Franklin. He's my brother." Trish lowered her head farther, fighting the aftershock faintness.

"Do you know if he has insurance?"

"He teaches school in Washburn." Trish's lips felt as if they were freezing up on her, making it harder and harder to reply.

The receptionist nodded. "Has he been a patient here before?"

"Yes."

"Do we need to do all this right now?" Grey asked.

"That's all I need. I can take it from here." The woman walked away.

Trish pressed her face into her hands. But the smell of blood was too strong. She looked up, responsibility nagging her. "I should call my dad."

"Wait until—"

Her brother's gurney was pushed out into the hall. "We're

on our way to surgery," the nurse who was rolling the IV pole called to her. "Notify his family." And then they were eaten up by the closing elevator doors.

Trish turned to Grey. "Please pray." She forced out the words through lips taut with fear. "I can't bear to lose him."

Grey nodded and bowed his head.

Stepping outside briefly, Trish punched her father's phone number into her cell phone and she gave the news to her younger brother who'd answered. Afterward, she returned to sit side by side with Grey—for how long she didn't know. Her gaze kept shifting to the silent man beside her. Now she noted that his blue-black hair was liberally threaded with silver. His eyes were gray, too. Now his head was indeed bent in prayer. Grey Lawson praying? But his words in the Jeep on the way here had resonated with honest faith. Her mind couldn't wrap itself around this idea. It just didn't fit.

The automatic doors parted and her family surged inside. Her father, Noah, and Andy's wife were at the front. "Trish! Where's Andy?" Noah barked. "Is he all right?"

Trish rose, grateful to see her family, but suddenly wary as if watching a match flare near a pool of gasoline. What if her father recognized Grey and demanded to know why she'd sat near him? She should have anticipated this and separated herself from him.

She hurried forward away from Grey, hoping to distract her father. "Andy's in surgery."

The receptionist stepped around the counter. "Why don't all of you go up to the surgical waiting area? After the surgery, the doctor will go there to report the patient's condition."

Trish shepherded her family toward the elevator, telling them about Andy's accident. As the door closed, she looked out. Grey Lawson had vanished.

IN THE HARSH FLUORESCENT LIGHTING, Grey examined himself in the men's room mirror. He looked like something out of a horror flick. He pulled his knit shirt over his head. Saturated and sticky with blood, it made a slapping noise when it hit the sink. He began rinsing it in cold water. Finally, it was blood free. After washing his face, hands and upper body over the small sink, he moved to the hand dryer and dried his body and then his shirt enough so that he could bear to put it on.

Worry about Andy Franklin nipped him. Why had this happened? He recalled praying the Twenty-Third Psalm in the Jeep. Why had he been thrust into the "presence of my enemies" as David had been? Was it a sign of what was to come, what he faced now? But most of all, what kind of woman was this Trish Franklin? A female deputy in Winfield? That was different. And had she really tried to give him a ride home? His impression of her, a neat feminine form and the way the top of her head had fit right under his chin, lingered in his mind.

Outside in the hall, he went to a courtesy phone and called his aunt. Her worried voice came on and he assured her he was okay but would be home later than expected. After her soft goodbye, he hung up and went out to the police Jeep. It was unlocked. He hadn't expected that, but had wanted to check first. He didn't want to go anywhere near Noah Franklin. Maybe Trish figured this was a safe area or maybe she'd been so shook up she hadn't thought of locking it. No matter.

He reached in the front seat and pulled out his duffel bag. The chill evening made him shiver. He shed the damp shirt and donned a T-shirt and another sweatshirt from his bag. Then he started walking. He had many miles to walk before he would see home tonight.

For a second, he recalled the glimpse of Noah Franklin, who fortunately hadn't looked his way. He thought of Trish Franklin again. What had possessed her to offer to drive him to his aunt's house? Noah Franklin was a hard man. Every soul in Winfield knew that. Helping Grey would pit Trish against her own father. Andy's little sister had guts all right. He'd give her that.

Grey had missed a bullet tonight. But he couldn't avoid Noah forever. Then again, he pictured the Franklin girl's bright copper hair under her deputy sheriff's hat. He hadn't recognized her at first. She was at least a decade younger than himself. He'd recognized Andy, though. They'd been in high school together.

So this was coming home. Seeing familiar faces once more and dreading what hostile words might issue from those faces. Sick dread at the thought of more of the same funneled through him. He quickened his pace. His aunt would worry till he knocked on her door.

WHILE HER FAMILY WAITED for the doctor, Trish went to clean up in the upstairs women's restroom. Watching the blood wash from her hands and face down the sink shook her. She pulled at her khaki deputy shirt where blood was making it stick to her body. She shuddered and took in air. How could she take care of getting Grey to his aunt's house? She didn't want to repay him for his assistance tonight with either a long chilly walk home or an unpleasant dose of her father's anger. And if Noah discovered Grey was here, that's what would happen. Maybe if she called the sheriff, he'd have someone pick up Grey and take him home.

Damp, but cleaner, she returned to her family—her other two brothers, her father, Andy's wife and Trish's godmother, Florence LaVesque, who was the sister of one of Trish's late aunts. Widowed, she and Trish's dad often fished and hunted together.

Now Florence looked up and asked the exact question Trish had wished to avoid. "What was that bad penny Grey Lawson doing sitting next to you in the waiting room?"

Every face turned toward Trish. There was a dazed silence in the room.

Trish stared back at her godmother, who was famous for always saying the wrong thing. Or at least almost always.

"Lawson?" Her father reared up. "Grey Lawson? *Here?* When did he get out of prison? Is he on the run?"

Trish's brothers shifted uneasily in their seats. Trish frowned at Florence. But her godmother had only spoken the truth, the truth that they'd planned to reveal tonight anyway.

Trish faced her father, who suddenly reminded her of a bull about to charge. "We—" she nodded toward her brothers "—were coming to tell you that Grey Lawson has been released on parole. And he's come back here to help out his aunt."

"Parole!" Noah began striding back and forth, his hands fisted.

"Yes, he's served seven years of his sentence." Trish recited all she'd dug up in the two days since the sheriff had received the letter, announcing Grey's imminent release. "And evidently Grey has been a model prisoner. The parole board had no problem in releasing him on extended supervision."

Her father began cursing under his breath.

Her next-oldest brother, Chaney, rose and tried to rest a hand on Noah's shoulder. "Dad—"

Noah pulled away like a petulant child. "What was Grey Lawson doing with you downstairs?" he repeated Florence's question, but coated each word with loathing.

Trish braced herself. "I'd just picked him up for hitchhiking when I came on Andy's truck."

"You were taking him in for hitchhiking?" Noah sounded pleased.

"No," Trish replied honestly, steeling herself, "I was taking him to Elsie's. I knew she'd be waiting for him—"

Noah's face turned red and he sputtered for words.

The surgeon in green scrubs strode down the hall toward them. "Franklin family?"

Penny Franklin rose and stepped forward. "I'm Andrew's wife."

"Your husband will be fine. The antler just nicked an artery. He's got abrasions and lacerations and he's bruised pretty bad. But a deer hitting a windshield can do a lot more damage. He was lucky someone was there. Someone that knew what they were doing and was able to get him here in time."

"Yes, Grey Lawson," Trish said, knowing how her father would react but unable to keep back the truth. "If Grey hadn't been there to help me, I couldn't have gotten Andy here in time."

Her father growled with intense incoherent anger.

The doctor looked from her to Noah, wary now. "The patient will be in recovery for a while." He held out a hand toward Penny. "Would you like to come and sit beside him?"

Penny assented and followed the surgeon. Trish turned and headed toward the elevator.

"Where are you going?" Noah demanded, his harsh voice slapping her from behind.

She stepped inside the elevator and then turned to face her father. "I brought Grey here and now I have to get him home to Elsie." The elevator doors closed, cutting off her father's furious reaction. Alone, she leaned against the rear wall. Let her brothers deal with their father. She'd done the worst task. She'd announced the fact of Grey's release.

Downstairs, Trish looked around for Grey in vain. Finally, she asked the receptionist, who said she thought he'd left. Trish hurried outside to her Jeep. She'd forgotten to lock the Jeep and Grey's duffel was gone. The mist had ripened into a heavy fog by now. Trish started her Jeep and headed down the drive toward the highway. She'd probably find Grey hitchhiking home.

The steering wheel was sticky and repulsive with her brother's blood. She reached under her seat and brought out a pack of antibacterial wipes. She used one on the wheel as she steered through the mist.

About four miles northwest of Ashford, she glimpsed Grey. His head down and nearly invisible in the mist, he looked just the same as when she'd picked him up on Cross-cut Road about three hours before. Trish slowed and pulled onto the shoulder, her blue lights rotating for safety. This time she didn't get out. She waited for Grey to realize it was her and come to the Jeep.

He opened the passenger door and paused. "I didn't think I'd see you again tonight."

"Did you think I'd make you walk all the way to Elsie's?"

"I thought you'd be detained at the hospital. How's Andy?"

The casual way Grey Lawson referred to her brother brought home to her that this man—though a stranger to her —was part of the fabric of Winfield, a stray thread that would now be reknit into the town. But with what repercussions and consequences? How would this all play out? "Andy's fine. Thanks to you. Get in."

Grey eyed her and then swung up onto the seat and slammed the door.

"Should I call Elsie?" Trish pointed to the cell phone charging on the dash.

"I called her from a courtesy phone at the hospital and told her I was running late."

"Okay."

Again, this man's presence filled the silent Jeep. She tried to keep her attention on the road. It was foggy and another deer could sprint across her path at any time. But her eyes kept sliding sideways, catching glimpses of the dour man so near, yet so removed. His jaw was firm. In spite of the seat belt, he sat shoulders forward, his hands folded over his knees. An invisible wall of history separated them.

The miles sped past. Trish was aware of the whizzing of her tires against the damp pavement and the clicking of crickets. Whenever they passed a small lake or stream, the song of frogs flickered through her open window. Finally, she turned down Cross-cut Road again. She slowed to the place where Andy's truck had been hit by the deer. The truck was still there, nose down into the ditch. But the buck was gone.

"The deer must have revived," Grey muttered.

He was right.

"That happens all the time," she commented flatly. "How they can get up after colliding with a pickup and take off is...amazing." Her emotions seemed to have gone into neutral. What she'd been dreading tonight and what had happened were so at odds that she didn't know how she felt right now. She turned down Slater's Road and then Ryerson's Road. She sensed Grey stiffening beside her.

Ahead, a log cabin, an old one, built of huge weathered logs, had many lights gleaming from its small windows. The battered roadside mailbox read Ryerson. Fog rolled over her windshield as Trish bumped the Jeep up the rutted dirt road.

The front door was thrown open. Elsie Ryerson stepped outside into the mist. "Grey! Grey!"

Grey opened his door; he turned back to Trish, but didn't meet her eyes. "Thanks." He shut the door and then he was hurrying up the few steps to Elsie, who clasped him to her. An old black-and-white-speckled hunting dog barked and jumped up and down around Grey and Elsie.

Trish watched, thinking of the welcome her father had given her when she'd moved back this spring. Two prodigals had returned. But Grey Lawson, the convict on parole, had received the warmest welcome.

———

SHE SAT BESIDE THE wall phone in her kitchen, staring at the floor. Finally, she realized that she hadn't moved since she'd hung up after Florence's phone call. She glanced at the clock. She'd been sitting here, brooding for almost an hour. She bent her head into her hands. In spite of what he'd done for Andy Franklin tonight, how could they just let Grey Lawson out of prison? It wasn't right. It wasn't fair.

And she wasn't going to stand for it.

Chapter 2

The next morning, Grey Lawson's first day back in Winfield, she put her plan in motion. She hadn't gotten much sleep the night before. But now determined, she drove off Bear Paw Road onto the old logging road. Glancing around, she was elated that there was no one on the road to see her turn down the private road to the hunting shack. She had to be careful and not give anyone a hint at what she planned to do. Suspicion must fall on Grey Lawson.

She jounced over the ruts left from many summer rains and pulled behind the old log shack where she and her husband had spent many deer and bear hunting seasons. Her throat swelled with emotions—sorrow, regret, anger—the ones she usually kept at bay.

It was all Grey Lawson's fault that she was feeling this way. He'd come back to town as if he had a right to. It wasn't fair. But she'd hit on a way to make him pay, make them send him back to prison where he belonged. The murderer.

GREY PARKED IN FRONT of the post office that morning. He helped his white-haired, plump Aunt Elsie out of the faded silver-green Chrysler and into the small crowded post office. Walking this close to her, he felt the "rolling" trembling that signified her Parkinson's disease.

"I see your nephew's with you today, Elsie." The woman behind the counter looked him up and down. She did not appear pleased to see him.

Grey's face warmed, but he kept his expression noncommittal.

"Yes," his aunt replied. "I'm so glad to have him back home again. A book of stamps, please."

———

THE DOOR TO THE LARGE shed, hidden by forest behind the hunting shack, creaked open. Dust floated in the morning sunlight. She grinned at the old gray sedan left there to molder. Just what she needed. No one had seen this car for years and it was faded the right shade. It would be almost invisible in the fog. Bending down, she reached inside the grill, found and released the hood latch. With a groan, the unlubricated hinges fought her as she pried open the hood. Donning work gloves, she then fished an old rag from her pocket to wipe the dipstick. Low as she'd expected. She went about adding oil to the engine.

She then hefted the old battery she'd brought along into place and connected it to the engine. With the red gas can from her truck, she added gas to the sedan's tank. The driver's side door opened reluctantly. Inside, she sneezed on the dusty interior and tried to start the car. Nothing. But she'd come prepared. She connected her truck and the sedan with jumper cables. Soon the engine ground to life. Disconnecting the cables, she let it run to charge the old battery.

So far everything had gone just as she'd anticipated. Now she just had to figure out her plan of attack.

━━━

TWO MORE PEOPLE ENTERED the small one-room post office. Grey knew that they would probably notice him. He would have gladly run these errands for Elsie. And without Elsie along, he would have been in and out. But his aunt was never one to stay home every day. He knew that she was thrilled to get out of the house today. Of all the things in this world he comprehended, he knew the feeling of being incarcerated, trapped. After so many years behind bars, Grey still felt shaky, almost fearful someone would tap him on the shoulder and drag him back to prison.

Walking free was something he'd never take for granted again. Shrinking back against the wall, Grey lowered his gaze to the floor as the two newcomers greeted the post office mistress and Elsie. He recognized their voices. How could that be? He hadn't heard his old childhood coach's voice for years and yet he could still pick it out.

"Grey."

Grey looked up.

Tom Robson held out his hand.

Grey felt his mouth go dry. He raised his own hand that somehow felt heavier than it should and grasped Tom's. He met the same strength there that he recalled from his days on Tom's youth football team.

"I'm so happy you've been able to come when your aunt needed you."

Grey looked up into Tom's eyes. "Tom." He managed to squeeze out the word.

"Looks like your aunt's going to have to feed you up some," Tom commented.

Grey fumbled for something normal to say back, but settled for a murmur of assent.

"Grey, Tom came out and gave my Chrysler a once-over last week," Elsie said and then her voice became conspiratorial. "Did I tell you he and Shirley Johnson are courting?"

Grey made himself join in the banter. "*Tom* found someone to court?"

Tom grinned. "Yeah, I'm a lucky man." He nodded at Shirley Johnson at the counter.

"Don't let this one get away," Elsie said, still in the low conspiratorial tone and smothering a grin. "Shirley's a keeper."

"You'll get no argument from me," Tom said.

"Good." Elsie looked up at Grey. "I need to stop at Ollie's and get milk and eggs."

Grey offered her his arm and helped her toward the door. Tom hurried ahead and held the door open so Grey could ease his aunt outside. Grey nodded his thanks as he escaped.

━━

SHE MENTALLY WENT OVER her plans one more time. After assuring herself that she'd foreseen every possible difficulty, she finally switched off the gray sedan's growling motor. She left the car and shut the shed door. She could go home now because she knew exactly what she'd do, when and where. It would do the trick, she was sure of it. Last night had been just the kind of night she needed. Would tonight be just as foggy?

Grey Lawson, you shouldn't have come back here. Then she thought of Elsie Ryerson needing help now that she was suffering the first stages of Parkinson's and her conscience pinched her. But she elbowed this aside. Right was right. And Grey Lawson walking free wasn't right.

GREY HELPED ELSIE INTO Ollie's Convenience Store to get the eggs and milk. There he got a surprise.

"Hey! Man!" Eddie Lassa, one of Ollie's nephews, hurried from behind the counter. "Great to see you!"

Grey felt his eyes moisten. But he was able to hide it as Eddie, his lifelong friend, pounded his back and then threw his arms around him in a big bear hug.

A pretty brunette walked past them out the door. She cast a mocking glance at them and stalked away.

Eddie grimaced and said something under his breath. Then he turned back to Grey. "I'm sorry I didn't write much, man. But you know me and English class." Eddie gave Grey a lopsided grin. "We'll have to get together."

Grey assimilated this in an instant. Still looking the same as he had in high school, buzz cut and all, Eddie had been his drinking buddy from the time they'd graduated together. After Eddie's warm welcome and in light of what Eddie had lost seven years ago, Grey had a hard time pulling words together. "I'd...like that. But Eddie, part of the conditions of my early release is that I attend AA twice a week. I can't even go near a bar."

"Hey!" Eddie punched his arm. "No problem. We'll go to Trina's for a pasty lunch sometime soon. Okay?"

"I'd like that." Grey had eaten only cold cereal for breakfast. Suddenly he felt empty, as if he hadn't eaten in ten years. That's what happened at the mention of Trina's flaky pastys, swimming in rich brown gravy.

"Oh, that sounds good," Aunt Elsie said, making a show of smacking her lips. "It's good we brought the cooler to keep the eggs and milk in. I'd love to have an early lunch at Trina's."

Grey's stomach dropped to his toes. He hoisted it back into place. "Let's do it." He might as well face the whole town down and get it over with. *Please, Lord, don't let some "righteous" citizen hurt her today because I'm with her.*

Elsie walked over to the doughnut case and began selecting a few. Eddie leaned close to Grey and spoke near his ear. "Do you think it was really a good idea coming back here? I mean, I'm glad to see you, but..." Eddie's voice faded away and he shrugged.

His aunt needed him and so he'd come back. "I thought of asking her to move with me somewhere else," Grey muttered, so softly that Elsie wouldn't hear. "And she would probably have said okay. But how could I do that to her? This is her home." Grey would never wrench Elsie from her lifelong friends, the shore of Lake Superior and the thick pine forests that she so loved.

"Yeah," Eddie agreed. "Yeah. I guess people will just have to get used to you being here. But it would have been better if you'd gone elsewhere."

Grey shrugged.

Elsie handed Grey the bag of doughnuts. He went and got the milk and eggs and paid Eddie. Grey had just turned toward the door when into the small convenience store walked Lamar Valliere. Grey held his breath and took his aunt's arm. This was one of the people who wouldn't be happy to see him in Winfield.

In jeans, a Packers jacket and with collar-length black hair, Lamar stood stock-still, watching them approach. Grey and Elsie reached the doorway that Lamar was blocking. With his dark brown, almost-black eyes, Lamar gave Grey a searing look. At the last possible second, he stepped aside.

Grey steered Elsie outside, grateful that Lamar hadn't said anything to hurt her. Lamar had suffered just as much or more loss in the tragedy seven years ago than Eddie. But Lamar didn't look the least bit forgiving. Not surprising.

With the eggs and milk and a few other items safely

stowed in the cooler in the backseat, Grey drove them to Trina's Good Eats, an institution in Winfield. The original 1927 bell above Trina's door jingled when Grey led his aunt inside. All eyes turned toward them as was to be expected. Grey spotted Trish Franklin in the last booth with a man who looked like Carter Harding, whom Grey knew was sheriff now.

Carter had had family problems, too, when he was growing up. But he'd been lucky. He'd had Tom Robson for a stepfather. Halting this line of self-pity, Grey twisted the end of his bitterness into a knot. He reminded himself of a painfully learned truth. No matter what his parents had done, he had to bear the responsibility of his own crimes. Not blame them on others.

While Elsie beamed at everyone in Trina's generally, Grey looked over everyone's heads and led Aunt Elsie to an empty booth near the back. The mixed aromas of roast beef and melted butter hung appetizingly in the air. Grey helped Elsie ease into the booth and then he slid in across from her, facing the door. The booth was the original high-backed, dark-wood bench with a worn matching table.

Grey sensed a change in the restaurant's atmosphere. Winfield was processing his homecoming. Would Trish and the sheriff feel the need to "notice him officially"?

A thin blonde in her middle years, Trina ambled over to the table. She eyed him but spoke to Elsie. "You have the look of a woman in need of one of my pastys."

Elsie chuckled. "You don't miss a trick. Grey and I both want your pasty special with extra gravy. We're celebrating his return. And I'm no cook anymore."

Trina patted Elsie's shoulder. "Iced tea or coffee today?"

"Two iced teas," Elsie replied.

Trina nodded and walked away, leaving Grey feeling simultaneously like the Invisible Man and a mannequin in a store window. Everyone watched him but no one caught his eye. So be it.

With sinking dread, he heard footsteps from behind. The law had decided to come to speak to him. Trish Franklin, deputy sheriff, and Carter Harding, sheriff, paused beside Grey. Grey tried to focus on Harding's face, one he recalled from their school days. He had to force himself to focus on just Harding's face, not on Trish's pretty face. With her hat off, her bright copper curls frothed around her face. *Off-limits*, Grey chided himself.

"Mrs. Ryerson," the sheriff said, "I see Grey's already got you gadding about."

Elsie glowed at Harding's friendly words. "We're celebrating his homecoming with pasty specials."

"Excellent." Harding nodded at Grey and in a soft voice said, "Your parole officer will report any violations of your early release to me. I don't want to hear boo from her."

Face flaming, Grey suppressed his sharp reaction to this public humiliation. He was a marked man and just because he was home again, didn't mean his life would ever be the same. "You won't."

"Good." Harding patted Elsie's shoulder. "Enjoy your pasties." He walked to the register to pay.

Trish leaned in and smiled at Elsie, but she spoke to Grey. "Thanks again for your help last night."

"No problem." His lower than usual voice scraped his throat. He tried to ignore how her honest eyes connected with his. Trish's eyes were a warm brown, like liquid milk chocolate. Unbelievably, her gaze was direct and free of blame. He had to clear his thick throat. "Thanks for the ride home."

"I want to give you a warning," Trish said, moving right on, sounding businesslike. "I know you haven't had a chance, but I noticed last night that your driver's license has lapsed. Get that taken care of today. Have someone drive you down to Ashford and get it renewed."

Grey nodded, glad she was only giving a warning. "I will."

"It's all right that he drove me here?" Elsie asked, obviously worried. Her trembling became more pronounced. "I didn't think. I didn't mean to get Grey into trouble his first day..."

Trish squeezed Elsie's hand. "He just needs to take care of it right away." She started to go and then halted. She turned back almost with an air of resignation. "I'm off duty today and I'm going to Ashford to visit my brother this afternoon. Why don't I pick you up in about two hours at Elsie's?"

Grey tried to analyze the pretty deputy's expression and tone. Her father and probably most of her family hated him. Why was she being so accommodating? Was she merely paying him back for his help last night? He'd only done what common human decency demanded. But maybe she didn't expect a felon to have common human decency.

"That's so sweet of you," Elsie accepted for him as he wrestled with a welter of reactions to the deputy's offer. "We'll be home by then."

Trish nodded and then walked to the register.

Trina arrived with their iced teas. She looked Grey up and down and lifted her eyebrow as if to say, "You're in trouble already?"

———

GREY SAT IN TRISH'S red SUV outside Ashford Hospital. Trish had picked him up as arranged and now he had his new driver's license in his pocket. But he'd demurred at going up to visit Andy, Trish's brother. When Grey said he'd wait in the car, Trish looked relieved. That wasn't surprising. What if Noah Franklin had been up there? Or arrived while Grey was with

Andy? He didn't want to think of the humiliating public spectacle that would have caused.

How could Grey make Trish understand she didn't have to be nice to him? He'd helped her last night because any human —even an ex-con—would find it hard not to help another human being in Andy's situation. Grey had met some in prison who wouldn't have, but only a few. He hadn't done anything special last night.

Someone tapped on the window and Grey jumped.

It was Trish. She opened the door. "Sorry to startle you. Andy wants to see you, to thank you."

Grey's face stiffened. "That's not necessary."

Trish implored him with her milk-chocolate eyes. "Come on up. He's alone and we'll only stay a minute. We'll tell him that I have to get you back to take care of Elsie."

Grey considered balking, but decided that would only take more time. He wanted, needed to get back to his aunt's house. Today had been grueling and now he had to face Andy. When would this chafed-raw sensation pass?

And from the pace she'd set for them, evidently Trish understood something of his desire to get home. He hustled along beside Trish into the hospital. She was power-walking him up to her brother. Maybe she was just as conscious of what would happen if her father walked in and found Grey Lawson with her and Andy. Grey didn't want to think of facing Noah Franklin. Trish entered Andy's room. Grey paused in the doorway.

Andy held out a hand. "Grey, long time no see."

That's one way to put it, Grey thought drily as he neared and then shook hands.

"It seems like a lot of years ago that we played high school football together."

Grey tried to come up with something to say and fell back

on something he'd overheard last night. "I hear you're a schoolteacher now."

"Yeah, science and math. It's a good life. I don't have to work outside like both our fathers did, logging."

Grey merely nodded. He didn't have anything he wanted to say about either of their logger fathers.

"My baby sister," Andy teased with a grin and chuckled when Trish stuck her tongue out, "tells me you were on the spot last night to help out."

"You would have done the same for—" he thought fast and substituted "—anybody." Instead of "me."

"I bet it's hard for you to come back...after all you've been through."

Grey shrugged, uneasy with sympathy and any possible mention of prison or what he'd done to get there. *I don't want to talk about it.*

"I won't keep you. Just wanted to thank you."

"No problem," Grey mumbled.

Trish leaned over and kissed her brother's cheek. "Bye."

"See you around then." Andy waved at them as Grey and Trish left together. They walked in silence to the car and then Trish drove them away.

Grey tried to ignore the way her presence permeated the vehicle. She was wearing a fragrance that smelled like spicy vanilla. And for her day off, she'd changed from her deputy uniform into jeans and a brown-and-blue-plaid flannel shirt. Though no one would have accused her of trying to catch male attention, her trim womanly figure transformed the masculine attire into something essentially feminine. Against the blue-brown of her shirt, her skin glowed like a fresh peach.

He made himself face forward. It was just all those years in prison among men. That's why he couldn't ignore her, couldn't take lightly being close like this to a woman. He'd have to make sure that he didn't let himself think it meant anything else. He hadn't come back to Winfield to start his life over. That was on hold. He'd come back to care for his aunt until she no longer needed him. Then with his extended supervision finished, he'd leave Winfield. Far away, he'd try to find someone and maybe have a life.

The miles back to Winfield spun past his window. And then Trish's SUV was rocking up his aunt's uneven drive. He'd have to order a load of gravel next spring. Too late this year.

He was just about to ease out and say thanks when Trish looked at him full in the face. "Don't worry. I know how much trouble my father would make for you if he saw us together. But today I knew you needed to get your license renewed and I was going to Ashford anyway."

She understood what he was thinking. In fact, she'd probably been thinking the same thoughts. Well, probably not the part about how good she looked in jeans and a flannel shirt.

He nodded. "Got it." Then he turned toward his aunt's door. Bucky, Elsie's hunting dog, barked and ran toward him. He paused to pet Bucky, who wriggled with pleasure. Grey tried to ignore how unwelcome it was to hear Trish drive away. He'd survived his first day home in Winfield. That's what mattered. Not his fleeting attraction to an attractive but forbidden woman.

LATE ON SATURDAY EVENING, five days since Grey Lawson arrived in Winfield, she sat behind the wheel of the old gray sedan. Her nerves quivered with anticipation and fear. "I can do this. I can," she repeated to herself over and over. But her hands on the steering wheel trembled as if she had Parkinson's just like Elsie Ryerson. *I can't think about that now. I have to do this for Jake.*

Fog rolled, swirled around the gray sedan, making the car

almost invisible. She had chosen this location for its relevance to Grey and his unforgivable crime against Jake. She'd parked off Bear Paw Road where it had all happened over seven years ago. No one would mistake the significance of this place. Now she waited to do what she must do.

She heard a vehicle approaching, but couldn't see it due to the mist. *Do it now*, she ordered herself. She eased out of Park into Drive and pulled into the center of the road. Trying to time it just right, she started forward straight down the center line, picking up speed. Right toward the oncoming vehicle.

Chapter 3

Trish and Sheriff Harding drove up the gravel drive through the heavy fog. They parked and then walked from their vehicles through the cool moist air to Elsie Ryerson's darkened house. A strange tightness wound itself around Trish's lungs. She didn't want to be here to question Grey Lawson. She could tell Carter didn't, either. But an event had happened and this was their job. *We don't have a choice.*

The sheriff knocked on the old plank door, and then waited. It was well after midnight. Elsie and Grey were probably sound asleep. But only a few minutes passed until the door opened a crack. "Who is it?" Grey asked.

Her tension constricting more, Trish waited for the sheriff to respond. *I don't want to do this.*

"Grey, it's Sheriff Harding and Deputy Franklin. We need to talk to you."

The door opened. Grey stood just inside the low-lit shadowy kitchen in gray sweats. "Come in," Grey said in a subdued voice.

Trish realized that he, too, must not want their visit to disturb his sleeping aunt. Trish and the Sheriff moved almost stealthily into the neat kitchen, closing the door gently against the damp night. Grey motioned them toward ladder-back chairs around the table. With a nod, the sheriff and then Trish eased into them. A faint trace of cinnamon hung in the air.

Grey sat down, facing both of them and murmured, "What's this about?"

Trish studied the shadows cast over his austere features by the only light coming from above the stove behind him. The essence of Grey Lawson beckoned her closer. She shifted on the hard seat.

"Where were you this evening?" the sheriff asked.

"Here." Grey eyed them with a visible wariness, but didn't ask them for more information.

Her face frozen into a noncommittal expression, Trish waited for the sheriff to proceed.

"You weren't out in your aunt's car tonight?"

"No." Grey's dark-lashed eyes sought hers.

She avoided his gaze, fought the urge to reach out and reassure this grave man. The stove clock ticked over another minute.

"Can anyone corroborate your alibi?" the sheriff continued.

"What's this about?" Grey repeated.

"Just answer the question please."

An invisible but very effective veil came down over Grey's expression and his face turned to granite before her eyes. "My aunt was with me all day and all evening." Grey's words rasped her taut nerves.

The sheriff nodded. "That's what I thought, but I had to ask."

Grey did not repeat his question a third time. Just sat immobile and silent. Waiting.

Sheriff Harding gave her the barest of nods.

"There was an accident tonight or rather—" she had to stop to clear her throat "—a near miss on Bear Paw Road."

At her mention of the road where his life had altered direction forever, Grey didn't change expression by even a flicker of an eyelash. But a frost iced through her. Lives had ended that night.

"One of our summer residents was on his way home from a restaurant," she continued, each word costing her effort as she tried to sound matter-of-factly professional. "The mist had already impeded visibility. A late-model sedan, either gray, silver-blue- or green drove toward him right down the center line. This took place at almost the same spot where...where your accident took place."

"Was he hurt?" Grey asked in a strained voice.

"No," the sheriff replied. "But your aunt can vouch for your whereabouts all of tonight?"

Trish exhaled deeply, trying to release the strain from this interrogation. She watched Grey process the muted accusation. He stiffened, drawing himself up straighter. His jaw hardened.

"So you think that I'd leave my aunt alone," Grey said with sharp sarcasm. "Take her car and drive back to the site of my accident and try to kill another innocent driver?"

"No." Trish's denial came quickly. Blood rushed to her face. She curled her fingers into her hands to keep them from reaching for Grey's sleeve. Why did she connect with him so much? Why did she want to touch this man?

"No," the sheriff agreed equably. "But you know that many people around here will unfortunately jump to just that conclusion. We came to question you so we can tell them you have an alibi."

Grey grimaced and looked toward the kitchen window, shrouded with gray mist. "Right," he muttered.

Trish knew that her father would revel in this latest occurrence. *What's going on here, Lord? This doesn't make any sense.*

"Is there something wrong?" Elsie's frail voice came from the hallway. She stepped into the kitchen in a worn flannel robe and slippers.

Grey hopped up.

Sheriff Harding rose, also. "Mrs. Ryerson, sorry we woke you."

"I sleep lighter and lighter all the time. What's wrong?"

Grey gently guided his aunt onto a kitchen chair.

The sheriff didn't sit back down. Reading this signal, Trish rose, too. "We were just checking with your nephew," the sheriff replied, "about his whereabouts this evening—"

"He's been with me almost constantly since he arrived home." Elsie glanced up at Grey who stood with a hand on her shoulder.

"That's what Grey told us," the sheriff said. "We just wanted to get his statement straight first, so unwarranted suspicion wouldn't fall on him."

Trish listened to this without letting her uneasiness color her expression. She and the sheriff said their farewells and walked out into the misty night again. Grey's presence still summoned her to turn back, to offer to let him rest his head on her shoulder. She could feel the phantom touch of his hair upon her cheek.

Trish wrenched herself back to reality. How effective would their attempt at averting unfounded suspicion be? People would probably think that Elsie would say anything to keep her nephew from going back to prison.

But they would be mistaken. If Elsie Ryerson said Grey had been home with her at the time of the near miss, that's just where he'd been. Trish had zero doubt about that. So that left the question, who wanted to cast guilt on to Grey by playing such a stupid, dangerous game?

With a queasy feeling, Trish wondered where her father had been this evening.

THE NEXT MORNING, SUNDAY, dawned gray and windy, one of those harsh fall days that hint at the winter to come. With each step Grey took up to the church door, his confidence shriveled. Aunt Elsie must also be under a similar strain because earlier she'd even asked if he'd like to visit a different church today. Grey had been tempted by her offer. But why postpone the inevitable?

This had been his aunt's church since she was a child; he wasn't going to make her change churches just because Noah Franklin was an elder here. Over seven years ago, why hadn't it occurred to Grey that everything he did reflected for good or ill on his aunt? *How could I have been so selfish?*

He tried to focus on the fact that he was once again coming into the Lord's house, a place where he could worship the God of forgiveness, the God of second chances. The God who had become his refuge and strength in prison.

Obviously in high spirits, Elsie waved at friends as they made their way up the aisle to his aunt's favorite pew. Grey tried to focus on the church and not the people. But the back of Noah Franklin's head drew his gaze.

As always, Noah was sitting on the aisle in the left front pew. In the pew behind him sat most of Trish's family. He could still name her four brothers, though only three were present. Andy, whom he'd met again on his first day back sat beside his wife. Missing was the next brother, Trish's second-oldest brother, Pete, who lived out of the county. Then came Chaney, just a few years older than Trish and then Mick, the youngest. Grey, Andy, Pete and Chaney had all been close in age. All of the Franklin men were built like lumberjacks and had red hair. Chaney glanced over his shoulder and froze when he saw Grey.

Grey looked down, avoiding Chaney's gaze as he led Elsie

to her accustomed pew. Just as he reached it, he couldn't help himself. He looked again at the Franklin family ahead and noticed that a few of their widowed aunts also sat in the family pew. Grey tried to recall their names. One was Harriet, Jake Franklin's widow. He'd never forget her. Florence, whom he'd glimpsed at the hospital, sat beside her along with Wilma, who owned the bed-and-breakfast, another Franklin relative. The women cast him dark glances; Trish an unreadable one.

Grey and his aunt sat down six rows behind them. He hoped none of the rest of the Franklins would look around again. The expression on Chaney's face had been far from welcoming. Grey sat low in his seat and wished he could blend unseen into the old oak pew.

The organ prelude ended and Grey noted that Sylvie Patterson, the local bookstore owner, still played the organ on Sundays. She must be nearing thirty just like Chaney, and she had kindly sent him books periodically while he did time. The service began. Grey found it harder and harder to concentrate on the opening hymns. Even when Grey was looking at the hymnal, the back of Noah's head kept drawing his gaze.

The hymn ended and Noah Franklin walked to the pulpit to read this Sunday's scripture. The older man looked like an Old Testament prophet, dressed in a black suit, tie and white shirt. Without looking at the congregation, he took out drugstore reading glasses and began reading the parable of the Unforgiving Servant, from the Book of Matthew.

"Then Peter came to him and asked, 'Lord, how often should I forgive someone who sins against me? Seven times?'

'No!' Jesus replied. 'Seventy times seven.'

For this reason, the Kingdom of Heaven—"

In the midst of the reading, Noah glanced up, gazing out at the faces before him. And then he abruptly stopped.

Silence. Everyone looked up from their pew Bibles. Their gazes followed Noah's and soon the whole church was staring at Grey. Caught in the older man's crosshairs, Grey froze. The silence went on. Wind brushing the windows was the only sound.

"You," Noah finally pronounced the single word accusation. "You."

SITTING WITH HER FAMILY, Trish felt as though she were standing beside a large gong someone had just struck. Her father's voice echoed and vibrated through her. Earlier, when she'd glanced back and glimpsed Elsie and Grey entering the sanctuary, she'd known that he would balk at Grey's presence. But not out loud. Not in front of the whole congregation. Not from the pulpit.

"Get out," her father ordered, his quivering hand pointing toward Grey. "Get out of this church."

The pastor, William Ray, looked stunned where he sat beside and just behind her father. Whispers flew around the sanctuary.

"Out!" Noah ordered.

Trish rose. She opened her mouth to object.

But Pastor Ray also rose. "Noah," he said sharply, "what are you doing?"

Noah stepped away from the pulpit and stormed down the steps and up the aisle.

Pastor Ray pursued Noah. Just as the older man reached Grey's pew, the pastor grabbed Noah's elbow and pulled him around. "What are you doing, Noah? You're disrupting the service."

Noah tried to shake the pastor's grip off, but couldn't. "Let me go. If this murderer won't leave, I'll make him."

Grey had risen.

Trish watched the color drain and then return to Grey's face, leaving it a blotchy red and white.

After another attempt at breaking the pastor's grip, Noah turned back to Grey. "Get out. I won't have you in my church."

Trish's breath caught in her throat. She couldn't decide whether she should join the threesome or hang back. Would she ease or worsen the situation? With her father, it was hard to predict.

"You do not own this church, Noah," Pastor Ray stated loud and clear. "You do not have the right to tell someone to leave."

"He killed my twin brother!" Noah shouted. "He has no right to sit in this church with decent people!"

Others rose in their pews. "Sit down, Noah. Please," someone said. Similar murmurs seconded this.

"Noah, anyone who comes into this church is a sinner and no sin is greater than any other," Pastor Ray stated. "Grey Lawson did not *murder* your brother. It was all a tragic drunk-driving accident and Grey has paid seven years in prison for his part in it." Pastor Ray looked up at Grey. "You are welcome in this church, Grey. I was happy to see you come today." He held out his other hand toward Grey.

Noah roared and finally wrenched himself free of Pastor Ray. "I won't have it! I pay your salary, Pastor!"

"Well, don't we all? Even Elsie?" Florence declared from the Franklin pew.

Others voiced support for this view. "You don't own this church, Noah Franklin."

Grey moved to leave. "I don't want to cause trouble—"

But Pastor Ray now wouldn't release Grey's hand. "You are welcome here and you will sit down." He looked at Noah. "And this service will continue. Noah, I believe you were reading today's scripture."

The three men stood in a tense tableau. Again, the sanctuary fell silent. Trish could hear her heart beating in her ears. Would her father listen to the pastor or escalate his vendetta?

At last, when Trish's tension had reached the point where she thought she couldn't stand it, her father charged down the aisle and out the church doors. They slammed behind him. Like a gust of December wind through pine boughs, sighs of shock and dismay rustled through the church.

Pastor Ray said, "Grey, your aunt told me that you had rededicated your life to Christ in prison. Is that true?"

Grey only nodded.

"Then let me extend to you the hand of fellowship." Pastor Ray clasped both Grey's hands in his.

"Thank you, Pastor."

Trish could hardly hear Grey's reply.

Pastor Ray urged Grey to sit back down. Then the pastor leaned over Grey to take Elsie's hand. "I know you've been waiting and praying for this day a long time, Elsie."

Elsie wiped her eyes with an old lace hankie and nodded.

The pastor then strode back up the aisle toward the pulpit. He paused by Trish. "I think it's time we had a woman read the scriptures occasionally. Trish, will you come up and finish the reading for your father?"

More whispering.

Nonplussed, Trish simply obeyed, following him up to the pulpit. Pastor Ray sat again in his chair and Trish tried to calm her cantering heart and lungs. She cleared her throat and lifted the Bible slightly. She began again.

"For this reason, the Kingdom of Heaven can be compared to a king who decided to bring his accounts up to date...one of his debtors was brought in. He owed him millions of dollars. He couldn't pay so the king ordered that he, his wife and children and everything he owned be sold to pay the debt. But the man fell down before the king and begged him..."

GREY LISTENED TO TRISH'S voice gain confidence, becoming stronger, surer as she read the story of the servant who'd been forgiven much but who hadn't been forgiving with another servant. Her bright hair gleamed in the pale autumn light and against the oak-wood and white-plaster interior. Dressed in fall colors, she radiated a warmth, a cheer that brightened the room. Like a warm flame, she drew Grey toward her—an antidote to the chill left by her father.

From Noah Franklin, he'd expected shock and hostility. But never a public confrontation during the worship service. *Did I do right in coming here, Lord? I didn't mean to cause a rift in Your body, this church.*

After church, Grey tried at first to hurry his aunt out and home, but gave up. It seemed that everyone in the congregation wanted to talk to him or Elsie or both. Everyone had an opinion about his homecoming, Noah, and this morning's event. Grey stood as a silent sentinel beside Elsie.

Out of the corner of his eye, he noted many of the Franklins leave by the far aisle to avoid him. Again, Chaney, with a little boy obviously his son at his side, glared at Grey. But Penny and Andy, who still looked pale and moved slowly, came around the pew to thank him again for his help the night of the deer accident.

Where had Trish disappeared to? Grey finally was able to get Aunt Elsie out into the aisle and turned toward the door.

Out of nowhere, Trish appeared, offering her hand to him. "I'm glad to see you here this morning, Grey."

He couldn't doubt her sincerity. What made Trish Franklin tick? "I'm sorry," he mumbled, "about your dad. And everything." He made himself let go of her soft hand.

Trish inhaled deeply, but merely shrugged. She patted Elsie's arm and spoke softly to her. Then naturally as if he'd never been away and they'd been friends forever, she joined them in walking toward the doors.

Grey could hardly wait to escape. Trish should know better than to be seen walking with him.

Shirley Johnson, Tom Robson and a teen wearing an old pea jacket whom Grey didn't recognize, met them just inside the double doors. Tom introduced the young man as Chad Keski, Shirley's foster son. "Grey, I wanted to ask you if you would help out with the local food pantry," Shirley said.

Grey was surprised to be asked. "Sure. What do you want me to do?"

"Right now we're gathering food to help many of our families get through the lean winter months when seasonal unemployment will start hitting people. We start biweekly distribution in mid-October. We have various drop locations around the county and we need another person to pick up the canned and boxed goods left at them. Would you be able to take up a route?"

"Sure."

"Yes, my old buggy is running great," Elsie said, smiling, "thanks to Tom. When are you two setting the date?"

Shirley blushed.

"Show her," Tom urged.

Shirley reached into her pocket and slid a diamond solitaire onto her ring finger. "Tom wanted me to wear it today, but I chickened out. I didn't want to cause a fuss."

Me, neither, Grey echoed in silence.

Aunt Elsie and Trish cooed over the ring as women do. Then Grey was finally able to get his aunt out into the furious north wind. He hurried her to the Chrysler and helped her inside. Trish went to her SUV and waved farewell to them. He made himself look away.

As he shut his aunt's door, he looked over the hood of the car and saw two of Trish's aunts still staring at him from down the street. Their sour, unfriendly expressions chafed him like the violent wind. They were Florence and her sister, who'd been married to one of Noah Franklin's brothers. Florence's earlier retort aimed at Noah didn't mean she'd forgiven Grey. She just didn't like Noah much. And Noah had had five brothers, all dead now. All had been older than Noah except his twin brother, Jake. Jake Franklin—the man Grey had killed along with Eddie's girlfriend in a head-on collision seven years ago when he'd driven drunk one night, one of many drunken nights.

—

SUNDAY EVENING

She slid behind the wheel of the hidden gray sedan. She'd almost decided not to try another game of chicken. After her first near miss, her weak heart had pounded for almost an hour. Nausea had hit her in violent waves. Afterward, she'd been so relieved that her "victim" had been one of the summer residents, a stranger to her. She didn't want to scare anyone she knew out of their wits. Now she decided that this couldn't be helped. She had to risk another game of chicken. She had to.

Because this morning Grey Lawson had had the nerve to come to church before God and everybody. It wasn't right. Just recalling it, she boiled with resentment, sour bile filling her mouth. Noah had stood up to him. But a fat lot of good that had done her. The murderer had stayed in his seat and afterwards been greeted like a returning hero.

So grateful for the fog, she started the rough-sounding motor and drove down the rutted road, rocking on bad shocks. She positioned herself at the same point off Bear Paw Road and waited, listening for oncoming traffic. The tourist season had slowed from summer, but she hoped for another stranger to come unsuspecting into her trap.

In her mind, she went through the maneuvers she'd planned. Out of the mist, she'd drive straight at the oncoming vehicle. And at the last minute, she'd swerve to her right since she figured most drivers would swerve to their right, as well. And then she'd drive on up Bear Paw Road around the bend and disappear down the old logging road and onto the forgotten grass road that finally led to her shed. Then she'd park the car—

She heard a motor ahead in the mist. She drove into position and began to gain speed. The other vehicle purred closer. Closer. Closer.

The other driver hit his brakes. His horn. She swerved to her right. He swerved to his left—not his right!

The oncoming car was dead ahead! She screamed and twisted the wheel.

Chapter 4

Sunday Evening

He'd barely closed the door of the hunting shack behind him when he heard a rough-sounding car motor growling closer. He cursed silently and on reflex, bent low to avoid being seen from the windows. Would whoever was coming see his pickup parked behind the row of fir trees? Then he remembered that fog draped the dark night. Good. But what would he do if they were coming in the shack? Why would anyone come here anyway? It wasn't hunting season yet. Wasn't there anyplace left where a man could go to be left alone?

He inched along low, crablike, to the windows toward the sound. He glimpsed the veiled glow of headlights and then heard a car door being opened and shut and then a wooden door scraped over ground and latched. He cautiously moved to get a better angle to peer out. He eased up an inch or two to see if he should make a break for it.

Suddenly out of the mist loomed the figure of a large person. Was it a man or a woman? The person was moving oddly, kind of bent over. What was wrong with the stranger?

He tracked the figure as well as he could through the night and fog, all the time preparing to head out the other way if the stranger looked as if they were going to enter the hunting shack.

Then he heard what sounded like a woman moaning. The damp air seemed to magnify the depressing sound. The stranger, who looked like a woman from her walk, paused and leaned against the wide trunk of an ancient maple tree. Was she having an attack? Should he go help out? Finally, the stranger straightened up and walked away, swallowed by the mist.

In a few minutes, he heard another smoother-sounding motor start up and drive away. What was going on here? And what was in that shed?

He sat down on one of the old musty-smelling bunks and thought all this over. Finally, he got up and walked to the door. Enough time had passed since the unidentified stranger had left and the fog looked thicker than ever. He walked outside, closing the door against critters and headed toward the old shed back in the woods. When he got close, he saw the fresh tire tracks, still visible from the dampness on the road. He paused only a moment before he unhooked the peg securing the rusty latch. He opened the creaky old plank door.

The smell of gasoline and oil greeted him. Mist hung around him, but leaning forward through the miserable gloom, he could make out an old gray sedan. What had he just witnessed?

⊏⊐

SUNDAY EVENING

Trish sat at her small kitchen table, a cold cup of tea in front of her. Out the windows, she watched through the fog the stretch of woods between her trailer and her father's house. Where had her father been gone all afternoon and evening?

Now Trish saw a glow of headlights through the mist and heard the rumble and tinny rattle of her father's aged truck. *I really don't want to confront him, Lord.* But this was the main reason she'd come back to Winfield this year. Her father was aging and he needed her. And tonight he needed a reality check. His performance at church this morning had made that clear.

She pushed herself to her feet, pulled on her slicker and ducked out into her SUV. It was of course ridiculous to drive the short distance to her father's place. But the mist was heavy and the ground between the trailer and the house was slippery, rocky and uneven. Tonight was not the time or place for a stroll.

Within moments, she pulled up to the old farmhouse where she and her four brothers had been raised. She walked to the door and knocked, announcing herself.

"Go away!"

She ignored her father's antiwelcome and opened the door and walked inside. "Good evening to you, too."

Noah glared at her from under his white bushy eyebrows. "Go home. I don't need you checking up on me."

She sat down at the old kitchen table and studied him across the cluttered tabletop. "That was quite a show you put on this morning."

"I said go away! Why do you think I need you around always checking on me—"

"I'm worried about you," Trish went on without paying any attention to his objections. "You're going to make yourself sick if you keep this up."

"My health is my affair. I can take care of myself."

Trish stared sadly into his eyes. In her mind, she went over all the times she'd needed a father and found herself facing this severe man who deemed it impossible to show love of any kind to anyone. Least of all his daughter.

She opened her mouth to reply to him and then stopped. Another motor was speeding up the drive. She leaned forward to peer out the curtainless window but the fog defeated her. Her older brother Chaney, tall and broad with the same red hair as hers, burst into the kitchen.

Breathing hard, he stopped, facing her and Noah. "I can't find Young Jake."

Trish leaped up. "When did you last see him?"

"He was playing with Andy's kids at my place. Andy picked them up. We talked a bit first. Then he drove off. I called Jake so I could pack him up and take him back to his mom. I couldn't find him, Trish. I looked all over my place and I've driven all around the roads near my place."

Trish reached for her cell phone.

Chaney grabbed her wrist. "I don't want to report this unless it's absolutely necessary. You know how Rae-Jean will try to use this against me when we have the final custody hearing."

Chaney and his wife had been separated for over six months and on the brink of divorce. Trish paused. "But what if somebody snatched Young Jake?"

"Somebody snatch a kid here?" her dad barked. "In Winfield?"

She frowned. "That's not likely. But fall color tourist season brings a lot of strangers up here. I'll come with you and we'll begin searching together. But this fog." She exhaled with exasperation. "It's going to make it hard. And I'm calling the sheriff and reporting it now. We can't let your marital problems with Rae-Jean endanger Young Jake. And in fact, not reporting it to the sheriff promptly could be used against you at the custody hearing, too."

"You got all the answers, don't you?" Noah sneered behind her. She ignored him. For some reason her pinning on a

Winfield badge earlier this year had increased her father's hostility toward her, almost as if it had spawned a rivalry between them.

Chaney ignored Noah, too. "Thanks, sis." He pulled her toward the door. "Come on. Since Jake's on foot, I've been up and down Cross-cut Road. But now I want to go north on Bear Paw. Would you go south? And be sure to check all the private lanes, okay?"

"But what if Young Jake has left the road?" she asked, the possibility yawning before her with horrible consequences. Lost in the woods wasn't a fairy tale—not with all the vast square miles of forested lands all around them.

Chaney gave her a tense glance and headed for his black pickup.

After calling the sheriff at home, Trish was driving slowly down Bear Paw south of her father's place. Was the fog lifting or was that just her imagination? Praying for Jake's safety, she kept her gaze sweeping both shoulders of the road, looking for Young Jake, born seven years ago, the year her uncle Jake had died and named for him. Since there was no such thing as a "little" Franklin male, he'd been nicknamed Young Jake.

Then she saw a car off on the shoulder. She hit her brakes and slowed, pulling up behind it.

Leaping out, she ran to the driver's side and peered in. The driver was slumped over the steering wheel. She wrenched open the car door and felt for his carotid pulse. She found it and he was breathing. She realized then that this car was quite near the same spot as Grey's long-ago accident.

And very close to the recent near miss. What was going on here? A mere coincidence? She shook her head as if resisting this new worry. No time to stand around thinking. She lifted her cell phone from her belt and speed-dialed dispatch and reported the accident.

She wished Chaney still had a cell phone, but Chaney's

paper mill job south of Ashford had ended just months ago when the mill had shut its doors. He'd canceled his cell phone contract to save money. She had no choice but to stay with the accident victim, secure the accident scene and wait until help came.

The near miss, Young Jake missing, now this accident, she felt as if matters were mounting, spiraling, spinning out of control. *God, take care of Young Jake. Let us find him. And let this accident be just a coincidence.*

The injured man moaned and shifted, evidently in pain. This brought her back to the problem at hand.

"Sir, you've been in an accident," she said. "Try not to move much. I don't know the extent of your injuries. I'm a deputy sheriff. I've called for help."

The middle-aged man lifted his head and blinked at her. "Some nut forced me off the road." He shook his head as if trying to clear it. "Someone in an old car. Barely missed him."

Great, just great. Had this been another game of chicken? If so, this time it had left a person injured. "Try to stay calm. Help's on the way." She patted his shoulder. Her ears strained to hear sirens. *Hurry up. Come on. Hurry.*

━━━

THE SUNDAY NIGHT NOW past had been long, dismally damp and frustrating. At just before eight o'clock on Monday morning, Trish stood between her brother Chaney and Sheriff Carter Harding at the front of the town hall. Young Jake hadn't been found. Men and women were gathering here to form teams of searchers. Sheriff Harding glanced at the wall clock. "Okay, let's get started."

Grey Lawson entered, but stopped just inside the door. He'd come in so quietly that not even the men at the rear turned around. She tried to ignore his presence, but she tracked him from the corner of her eye. Grey moved to stand behind Tom. That was well away from Hank Valliere and his son Lamar and also from Trish's brothers and their wives and assorted relations who'd grouped around Chaney near the front.

No one else appeared to realize Grey had arrived, but her awareness of him zoomed to maximum effect. Probably because she was weakened by lack of sleep and worry. And not just worry about Young Jake. Tensing, Trish sent a quick prayer heavenward that Noah would remain unaware of Grey's arrival. A public scene between Noah and Grey would just about finish what was left of her stamina and her patience. She forced her gaze away from Grey, a harder task than she would have predicted.

Sheriff Carter raised his hand and motioned for silence. Everyone hushed. "Many of you have taken part in past searches," Carter began. "I want you to move through areas in an unbroken line so that if Young Jake is unconscious, we won't miss him. We're going to start along County N and sweep south to Cross-cut where Chaney Franklin's house is. If we don't find the boy by then, we'll break up into small groups and move east, west and south in organized search parties."

"I heard there was another game of chicken on Bear Paw last night," Florence LaVesque queried.

Dread for how this might affect Grey shivered its way through Trish. She couldn't help herself as she sought Grey's face. His expression was hooded. Who wanted to cause him more trouble? Who might be stacking the deck against Grey?

"A motorist was forced from the road last night," Sheriff Carter replied in a repelling tone. "He's at the Ashford hospital with minor injuries. Bear Paw Road has been blocked to all traffic around the scene of the accident. Two of my deputies have been on guard there all night and we'll begin gathering evidence as soon as daylight permits. I thought, and you agree I'm sure, searching for Young Jake was more urgent than—"

The doors burst open and Chaney's wife, Rae-Jean, a pretty and now disheveled blonde, rushed inside. "Why didn't anyone call me?" she shouted, charging toward Chaney.

"I did call you!" Chaney yelled. "Where were you?"

"That's none of your business. I'm not your wife—"

"Yes, you are—"

"Mrs. Franklin," Carter interrupted in his no-nonsense voice, "you were called. We left you several messages on your cell and home phone."

The sheriff's words stopped Rae-Jean in her tracks. She flushed and bit her lower lip.

He motioned her closer and then spoke quietly so that Trish right beside him had to strain to hear him. "And an Ashford officer even stopped at your house. No one answered his knock. We don't have time to discuss your whereabouts here and now," the sheriff murmured, obviously warning her that her negligence definitely would be investigated. "We need to get out and find your boy."

Rae-Jean covered her mouth with her hands. Trish had been shocked that they hadn't been able to contact Rae-Jean last night. Trish hated to think the rumors about Rae-Jean's alleged drug abuse and infidelity could be true. She hadn't understood why Rae-Jean had left her brother in the first place. But now Trish's heart murmured soft words of comfort to her.

Noah hissed, "Hussy."

Carter looked out over the men and women volunteers. "Everyone, let's gather at County N and Bear Paw and then we'll get started."

Rae-Jean burst into sobs. Shirley Johnson and Florence went to her and put their arms around her.

Chaney stomped up the center aisle, steering around his estranged wife and headed out. Trish followed him. Her family's suffering continued unchecked. Andy's accident had started everything; then Grey's early release had set her father off, and now Young Jake had gone missing. Who had put her family up on the dartboard?

Outside, Trish climbed into her SUV. For a moment, she rested her weary head back against the headrest. A night without sleep and one family crisis after another had left her drained. Grey appeared at her window. She rolled it down. "Hi." She tried to smile, but her lips quivered. With effort, she kept her hand from reaching for his.

Grey handed her a thermos. "Elsie made coffee."

The whole horrible night balled in Trish's throat and threatened to turn into tears. She fought to control her trembling lips, pulling together the trace of a smile. "Just...what I needed."

He pulled a plastic bag and a paper napkin from his jacket pocket. "And here's one of her cinnamon rolls. She knew you probably hadn't eaten anything since yesterday."

"I haven't but..." She looked over her shoulder at all the cars and trucks pulling out and driving away.

"I'll drive," Grey said, opening the door and nudging her to move over, "while you eat and drink."

She knew she should object but she didn't have the strength. Besides, everything within her clamored to have Grey near. *I shouldn't feel this way, but I can't help myself.* She slid over and let him take the driver's seat. She twisted off the red cap from the vintage plaid thermos and poured steaming coffee into it. Then she opened the sandwich bag and let the fragrances of butter and cinnamon soothe her and whet her groggy appetite. She sipped the strong brew Elsie always made and took a healthy bite of the roll.

"You've had an awful week," Grey commented.

"Tell me about it," she muttered, concentrating on eating the roll. Or trying to focus on it.

"Don't worry. We'll find Young Jake."

He stated the words with unmistakable assurance. These words, plus the coffee and roll, revived her strength.

Those were the last words they exchanged for the duration of the drive. She watched his sure motions as he drove, studied his blunt, competent fingers, his long sinewy arms. Unlike the men in her family who turned out tall and broad like lumberjacks, Grey had the lean build of a runner. Their quiet ride settled her nerves and the hot coffee woke her finally and fully.

The ride to the rendezvous point was not too many miles out of Winfield. Trish was chewing the last of the roll when Grey parked the red SUV with the others on the shoulder of County N. She gave him a confident smile.

He nodded in return and handed her back her keys. "Don't worry about me. I'll grab a ride with Tom back to Elsie's Chrysler."

"Right," was all she could say in return. Caution and her respect for Grey's reticence trapped words of thanks deep within her heart.

As Trish and Grey joined the others who were forming a search line on the southern shoulder of the road, the sheriff caught up with them. "Trish, you and I are going to head over to the crime scene. I've called the deputies that have been guarding the area around last night's accident. We're going to relieve them. When we arrive there, they'll come here."

Trish didn't know how she should feel about this order. Technically, she was off duty today and she really wanted to join the search. But solving the mystery was important, too. A multitude of emotions vied for her attention. Instead she merely nodded and handed Grey the thermos.

"No, you keep it." He held up his hands. "I had breakfast before I came."

Then he was off, taking a place in the string of men and

women who were waiting for the signal to begin sweeping through the forest south of County N.

Trish glimpsed Eddie Lassa nearby, who had hailed Grey. She made herself return to her SUV, though her every impulse was to stay at Grey's side till Jake was found.

Very soon she arrived at the scene of last night's game of chicken on Bear Paw Road. Dawn had burned its way through the lingering treetop mist. Bright yellow barricades still blocked the road from both directions. Without a word, the sheriff and Trish began their meticulous examination of the crime scene. He took one side of the road, she the other. She walked along the edge of the pavement, not wanting to disturb the soft gravelly shoulder, which might still harbor clues. She picked up a fallen branch and used it to stir the leaves.

After no sleep all night, she heard herself breathing in the cottony quiet of the still misty dawn. Only miles away, the search party was painstakingly, inexorably moving south toward them. Trish tried not to think of Young Jake huddled in the damp woods. *Help them find him, Lord. Show them the way to rescue him.*

The memory of the unpleasant confrontation between Chaney and his wife at the town hall lingered, bedeviling her. What happened to turn a husband and wife so sour toward each other? Had it been Chaney losing his job? Certainly not. Rae-Jean couldn't be that shallow.

With the stick, Trish nudged aside more fallen leaves, looking for anything that had come from a human being or a car. Inexplicably, her mind drifted back to Grey driving her to County N. How did he manage to captivate her? Why couldn't she just ignore him?

Was it because, just like at Andy's accident, he'd brought her exactly what she'd needed? This time it had been sustenance and reassurance. The simple kindness of hot coffee, food, driving—taking care of her for a short while—had comforted her. Grey somehow projected a strength that had made her feel stronger.

"Trish!" Carter shouted. "Come here!"

Trish jogged over to the sheriff, who'd begun searching the opposite side of the road. When she got there, she saw that he was pointing to a hubcap that had come to rest against a tree trunk.

"See here." He pointed downward toward the fresh imprint of the hubcap's trail through the damp soil. "If this is from the perpetrator's car, this could be just what we need." The sheriff spoke with satisfaction.

Trish hoped that this was true. Something had to start going right. She pointed to the ground where the hubcap had creased the road's shoulder. "It looks fresh and that track where it rolled is definitely fresh." She wished she could feel some lift from this discovery. But the search for Jake dominated her mind.

Carter touched her shoulder. "We'll finish up here and then join the search. We'll find your nephew. Don't worry."

She tried to let his confidence rub off on her. But inside an ache had begun, an ache to hold Young Jake close and feel her family whole again.

GREY PICKED HIS WAY through the forest, looking for signs that a little boy might have passed this way. About two arm lengths away, Tom Robson walked on one side of him while Eddie Lassa walked on the other. It was as if they were buffering him from the Franklins and Vallieres. This set off opposing feelings in Grey—one was thanks for their friendship and one was irritation. He shouldn't need their protection.

Farther down the line, Chaney forlornly called his son's

name on and off. Grey wondered what it must feel like to have a son in danger, to lose a wife. This morning it had been hard for him to watch Trish drive away with the sheriff. Her acceptance of his small help on the way to the search had meant more to him than he cared to voice. As she had left, a sensation of loss had stabbed him. *Keep your mind on the search,* he ordered himself.

He began again to pray for Young Jake's safety and that the search team would find him sooner rather than later. The sky had cleared to an unremitting blue. With no cloud cover, the weather was turning chilly and the kid would be wet from the rain and fog all night. It made the perfect recipe for hypothermia.

God, let us find Jake, he repeated over and over. But all he saw was the tall pine trunks, golden maple leaves, frost-shriveled ferns, pine needles and cones. All around chipmunks and squirrels rustled through the undergrowth and scampered up into boughs. Chaney's plaintive calls filled Grey with an intense feeling of loss, the kind of loss he might feel if he were Jake's father.

TRISH AWOKE WITH A START. She felt groggy and disoriented. There was a knock on the door of her trailer. A voice called her name softly, urgently. Still dressed, she sat up on her couch. "Coming." She yawned and staggered to her feet.

It hit her then. Young Jake hadn't been found. *He's still out there, Lord.*

She glanced at the stove clock. It was nearly midnight. After sundown, the search had been called off till daylight. She'd come home and sat down. Exhausted, she must have fallen instantly asleep. Now she opened her door.

A chill wind blew inside. Grey looked back at her in the

light from her outside lamp. "Do you have something of Young Jake's?"

For a moment she couldn't put it all together. Her mind felt like an unlubricated machine. She looked away as she yawned once more.

"You're dead tired, aren't you?" Grey moved inside and urged her back onto the sofa. "Maybe I should have waited till morning, but Bucky was making a commotion—"

"Bucky?" she asked, trying to make sense of Grey's words. Then the previous night and day—Jake going missing and finding another accident on Bear Paw—raced through her mind on fast-forward.

"Bucky. Elsie's hunting dog. He's old and that's why I didn't think of it during the day when the search party went out. He was a good tracker in his time—"

"Grey, you're not making any sense." Trish yawned long and hard.

Grey gripped her arms. "I know, but tonight about an hour ago, he started barking and wanting out. I tried to shut him up and then my aunt said maybe he heard something. I was thinking bear, so I turned on the yard lights and started playing music on the kitchen radio with the window open. Trying to scare the bear off, you know. Can't have a bear settling on our property for the winter. Oh, sorry." He released his hold on her arms.

His hands had been warm; now she felt a chill on her arms. *Bucky? Bear?* Her mind was on Pause and she couldn't seem to switch it to Play. "You're still not making any sense." Grey's chin showed stubble of new growth. As she gazed at him in the dim light, she imagined stroking his chin, letting its stubble rasp against her palm.

"Trish, after a few minutes of trying to scare off a bear, I began to wonder if maybe Bucky had heard not a bear, but a little boy. Do you have something of Jake's? It would help

Bucky find him. It's not impossible for Jake to have wandered near Elsie's place. He might be hiding from us."

"Hiding?"

"He might have hidden from the searchers. He ran away and now he thinks he'll be in big trouble. Kids don't think straight."

Trish came fully awake. "You might be right." She looked around even though she knew it was a wasted motion. "I don't have anything of Jake's."

"Will you go to your brother's and get something?"

Trish stood up. "Yes. Let's go."

Grey halted by the door. "I'll wait at my aunt's and don't tell them it's me that wants something of Jake's. Just let them think it's your idea, okay?"

His refusal to come with her threw her off balance. "The sheriff has asked the state to send dogs. They'll arrive by tomorrow morning."

"You want to wait till then?"

"No." She pulled herself together. She was an experienced deputy sheriff. She didn't need Grey to go with her. "I'll go get something from my brother and meet you at Elsie's."

Grey left without another word.

Trish hurried to her car, resisting the almost overwhelming urge to depend on Grey. *What's going on in my head? More importantly, will this work?*

In less than an hour, Trish reached to knock on Elsie's door, but it opened before her hand touched it.

"Did you get something?" Grey asked, holding on to Bucky's collar. The dog whined, trying to tug Grey outside.

"Yes, I told Chaney it was for tomorrow when the state dogs arrive." She handed Grey a small, somewhat grimy white sock.

"How's your brother doing?"

"He's feeling rough. We all are."

"Trish, is that you?" Elsie came up behind Grey and opened her arms.

Trish allowed Elsie to hug her. The soft, lavender-scented woman enfolded her. With resolution, Trish pulled away toward the door. "Let's go."

Grey was ahead of her, hooking a leash to Bucky's collar and letting the dog sniff the sock. "Right."

Chapter 5

From equal parts worry and chill, Trish shivered as she followed Grey through the pitch-black forest. Bucky howled his eagerness, straining at the leash, but Grey held him in check, moving slowly. The sky tonight was clear with only a few stars and the barest fingernail of a new moon. A strong front, with a high-pressure system, had blown in from the west, chilling them but saving them from another foggy night.

Both she and Grey carried large lantern-type flashlights that Elsie had provided. This far from the village lights, the darkness swallowed these small beams as if they weren't even there. If she turned off the flashlight, she literally wouldn't have been able to see her hand in front of her.

Trish realized that she was concentrating on the light moving over the ground and each of her footsteps because she didn't want to think about Young Jake, shivering alone and frightened in this impenetrable darkness. It was too painful.

She fought the fatigue that threatened her consciousness. Not even the rush of excitement over this new possibility lifted her weariness. Over the span of two very stressful days and nights, she'd had only a couple hours sleep. One footstep after another, she slogged after Grey. Even in the penetrating chill, she longed to lie down on the pine needles and leaves and go right to sleep. *God, is this a wild-goose chase?*

But she couldn't give up. As long as Grey shouldered on, she would follow him and his hunting dog. Young Jake must be found and tonight was better than tomorrow. *God, please let us find him tonight.*

Minutes, minutes, minutes passed. Trish clung to consciousness with slippery fingertips. She stumbled on a leaf-concealed fallen tree. Grey swung around in time to prevent her from landing on her face in the damp shriveled ferns and yellow birch leaves beneath her lantern light. "Thanks," she gasped.

"You're falling-asleep-on-your-feet exhausted," he said, sounding disgusted. "I should have had enough sense to leave you with Elsie."

"No, couldn't," she objected around a betraying yawn. "Young Jake doesn't know you."

Grey pulled her closer.

Bucky took advantage of Grey's momentary lax hold on the leash and charged off, baying loud enough to wake everyone within a mile.

Grey raced after the dog, shouting at Bucky to come back. Trish hurried after them. A low wet branch slapped her face. She blinked back tears of weariness and pain. She caught up with Grey suddenly, running into him. She clutched the back of his sweatshirt to keep her feet under her. Grey swung around and pulled her under his arm. Bucky had treed something. A possum? Grey barked a command at the dog and Bucky broke off in mid howl.

Leaning against Grey, she heard it then—whimpering, a child was whimpering. "Jake," she called, her voice loud in the stillness. "Young Jake, it's me, Auntie Trish."

"Auntie," a small voice quavered from above.

"Oh, Jake!" Trish exclaimed. "Oh, Jake!" Tears poured from her eyes as astounding relief arced through her like electricity. Grey gently settled her against a nearby maple. She gasped as if she'd sprinted all the way there.

Moving under the vaulted oak, Grey flashed his lantern high. "Young Jake, I'm here helping your auntie. Why don't you just jump into my arms?" Grey's voice sounded soothing and confidence-inspiring at the same time. "I'll just put down my flashlight. And don't worry. I'll catch you safe and sound."

Grey set the lantern on its bottom so its beam was cast skyward. He handed her the end of Bucky's leash and then held his arms up, ready. "Come on, Jake," he coaxed. "Just let go and jump down like a big boy. I'll catch you."

"I want my daddy."

"We'll take you right home to him," Grey assured the boy.

"I'm scared," Jake whimpered again. "I don't want to get a spanking."

"No one's going to spank you," Grey said soothingly. "Everyone's been worried."

"Mama spanks me when I bother her. She's going to spank me!" The little boy began crying in a desperate, out-of-control way.

"No one's going to spank you, Young Jake," Grey said. "Now come on. You're a brave boy. You even climbed a tree. You can jump down here. I know you can."

"Promise...you won't...drop me." Young Jake's question was interrupted by sobs.

"Word of honor. Now *jump!*" Grey commanded.

Jake dropped out of the tree right into Grey's open arms. Trish rushed forward and wrapped her arms around Grey, sheltering Jake within their embrace. She sobbed, unashamed.

"Auntie, you're getting my face all wet," Jake complained at last from the nest of arms.

She laughed aloud. "Sorry." Her heart rejoiced, wordless praise to God burst forth and echoed inside her.

Grey hefted the boy onto his shoulders piggyback style. Trish leaned against Grey, laughing with a trace of hysteria and gasping for breath. Grey put his arms around her as if transferring his energy to her. "Come on. Let's get this boy home."

She wished that she could just stand there in the warm cradle of his arms, his strength all around her and fall asleep. But of course she couldn't. She pulled away, picked up Grey's lantern and handed it to him. With the loop end of Bucky's leash around her wrist, she walked through the night quietly rejoicing. At her side, Bucky snuffled the ground in a contented way.

Soon they were in Elsie's kitchen. Trish phoned dispatch with the news of finding Young Jake. She then asked Grey to put the boy into her car.

"No," Grey replied. "You're too tired to be driving. I'll drive your car and tomorrow we can figure out how to get it back to you."

She started to argue with him, but stopped. Exhaustion made her agree. "Okay. Drive us to Chaney's house on Cross-cut."

"You're taking me to Daddy?" her nephew asked. "Not Mama?"

"We're taking you to your daddy's cabin," she replied.

"Good."

Young Jake's not wanting his mother—especially after this ordeal—worried Trish. Rae-Jean and her treatment of her son was something Trish would have to look into as soon as possible. These signs of possible abuse couldn't be ignored. She patted Jake's shoulder and followed Grey, who carried the boy out to her SUV.

Within minutes, Grey pulled up in front of Chaney's log

house. Several cars were parked in the wide space in front and the inside lights were still on. Trish got out and turned to get Jake out of the backseat. She paused when Grey didn't get out, too.

"I'll let you go in without me," Grey said. "In fact, don't mention me if you can help it. I'm not...very popular with your family."

"Grey," she began to argue.

"I'll wait here. Chaney will have to drive the boy in to the hospital to be checked over. When you come out, I'll drive you home. You need to get home and go straight to bed." His final words were stern, giving her an order.

One corner of her mouth lifted at this. But she was too worn-out to contradict him, especially when he was right. As she walked, hand in hand, with Young Jake toward the house, her mind flatlined.

All she wanted to do, needed to do, was turn Jake over to Chaney. The burst of adrenaline that she'd gotten upon finding Jake had vanished. She felt empty inside, as if she might fold up at any moment like a broken lawn chair.

She didn't knock. She walked straight into the bright kitchen and found Andy and Chaney drinking coffee at the table.

Chaney leaped up and staggered. He snatched his son into his arms and buried his face against Jake's cheek, sobs muffling his words of welcome.

Eyes wide, Andy stood up. "Where did you find him?"

Trish struggled with herself. Grey didn't want anyone to know, but how could she keep his part in this secret?

"Daddy, a dog found me," Young Jake said, words pouring from his mouth. "He scared me when he was barking under me. But he found me. I climbed up a tree. I'm sorry, Daddy. I just didn't want to go home to Mama. She's not nice sometimes. She yells at me. Don't let her spank me. The man said you wouldn't let anybody spank me."

"Man?" Andy asked, pinning Trish with a questioning expression.

"The man with the dog that found me," Jake answered. "He catched me when I jumped from the tree. I don't want to go to Mama. Please." And then the little guy slumped against his dad's shoulder.

"Get a blanket," Trish ordered. "I'll get him a juice box."

Andy rushed to obey and returned with a homemade granny-square afghan. He folded it around Jake. "Come on, Chaney. We need to take Young Jake to the ER and have him checked out. He's probably suffering from hypothermia."

They both moved, grabbing jackets off pegs on the way out the door. Andy led Chaney toward his vehicle. Then he turned to Trish. "What man with a dog?"

"Grey Lawson," Trish said and then lurched to the SUV where Grey awaited her. Dissembling took too much effort and why shouldn't people know Grey had found Young Jake anyway? Not even her father could turn this against Grey. *Right?*

TWO DAYS LATER, JUST before noon, Grey pulled up outside the community church. Aunt Elsie wanted to attend the biweekly community congregate meal.

"Now, Grey, don't hurry back. We always play a little pinochle after lunch," his aunt said with her hand on the door handle.

He got out and opened her door. "Don't worry. I won't deprive you of your pinochle." He grinned.

Aunt Elsie patted his cheek and hobbled to the curb. She paused there. Grey shut the door behind her.

"Grey, I need help." Elsie's voice was unhappy.

He came up behind her. "What's wrong?"

"You'll have to help me in. All of a sudden, I feel very unsteady."

"Maybe I should take you to see your doctor." He put one arm around her waist and positioned his other arm under hers, prompting her to lean on it for support.

"No. This happens sometimes. Once I get inside and sit down, I won't have to get up until I'm ready to go. Florence will fill a plate for me from the buffet."

Grey didn't like this but decided that he'd tell Florence to call him at Trina's if he were needed back early. Entering the side door, Grey helped Elsie down the six steps to the basement fellowship hall. He smelled turkey and sage stuffing in the air. Sunday school children's crayon drawings of fall leaves and trees decorated the old stone foundation walls. The old beige-speckled linoleum was polished to a bright shine.

He led Elsie to the table she preferred and helped her sit down on the old wooden folding chair. Glancing around, he saw Harriet Franklin glaring at him from another table. He looked away and located Florence in the church kitchen doorway. He started toward her.

Suddenly Hank Valliere was in his face. "I don't care if you did find Young Jake Franklin. I think you've got a lot of nerve to come back to this town. You're not wanted here."

Grey felt his face blaze. What could he say? Hank had lost his daughter Darleen in the accident that had also killed Jake Franklin and sent Grey to prison.

To make everything even friendlier, Noah came up to stand beside Hank. "Don't think that finding my grandson settles the score."

Grey turned and headed to the door. He didn't want a public scene to ruin his aunt's afternoon out.

"Everybody thinks we ought to be grateful to you," Noah

called after him. "But to me, you're just plain bad luck. First, Andy gets hit by a deer and then Young Jake goes missing. None of this would have happened if you'd stayed in prison!"

"Where you belong!" Hank added.

Grey ran up the six steps, embarrassed and baffled by Noah Franklin's twisted logic. Just outside the door, Grey encountered Pastor Ray, who grabbed Grey's hand. "God bless you for finding Chaney's son."

Grey ignored this. He hadn't done anything anyone else wouldn't have done. His concern was for his aunt. "Pastor, I'll be at Trina's having lunch with Eddie Lassa. If my aunt needs me, call me there."

Grey didn't wait for the pastor's agreement. He headed straight for the Chrysler, praying that his aunt hadn't been too embarrassed by the dustup with Hank and Noah.

Soon, Grey opened the door to Trina's, jingling the same old bell. It was hard to face people after what had just happened, but he wouldn't miss lunch with Eddie. Just inside the door, he looked around for Eddie, who waved at him from the last booth at the rear. Grey headed for him, looking over the other customers' heads. *Everyone, please ignore me.*

"Grey." Penny Franklin popped up from her chair and stopped him. "I'm so glad to see you so I can thank you for finding Young Jake."

"I didn't do anything but follow my dog," Grey muttered, easing sideways around her.

She didn't let him pass; she grasped his hand with both of hers and squeezed it. "Thank you. Thank you."

He nodded, red-faced, and moved around her. But he was blocked again. Two more citizens rose to thank him for finding the Franklin boy. This continued all the way until he reached Eddie and slunk into the booth. Why couldn't people just ignore him?

"Well, well, if it isn't the hero of the day," Eddie greeted him.

"Knock it off," Grey muttered. "I know I'm an ex-con but anybody would have done the same if their dog had acted like Bucky was."

"Hey, let them thank you. There's nothing wrong with being a hero."

Trina appeared beside them with the coffeepot in hand. "You two ready to order?"

"Two pasty specials. My treat," Eddie ordered.

"Grey's pasty is on the house," Trina replied, pouring them both coffees. "So glad you found the little kid okay."

"No, Trina," Grey objected, feeling a bit desperate, "that's not necessary."

Trina pointed her finger into his face. "No argument. Anything else I can do for you? The last time you were in here, Elsie mentioned you were looking for handyman jobs. I think I know of a couple of people looking for someone. Would you like me to write down their phone numbers for you?"

Grey felt churlish for the way he'd reacted to Trina's offer of a free lunch. Now she was offering him some work. "Thanks. That would be great. I don't want to live off my aunt."

"No problem. Say, Eddie, I hear that Miss Priss is still making life miserable for Ollie."

Grey glanced at her questioningly. Who was Miss Priss?

"Ollie's granddaughter Tanya who came back this year." Eddie supplied the answer. "You probably don't remember her. But you saw her that first day you were back in town. That pretty brunette with the bad attitude."

Grey tried to picture her but only came up with a vague image. "Was her mother Dee?" Grey asked.

"Yes, Tanya is Ollie's daughter's girl," Trina said. "Dee left Tanya's father for a well-heeled summer resident when Tanya was just a little kid. Now her mom's divorced and remarried again. Tanya's new man didn't want the kid around, so Dee sent Tanya here to her grandfather. Poor kid. But she's getting a bad rep, underage drinking and running around with anything with a tattoo."

"Yeah, I've had to work with her a few times. She's something all right," Eddie said.

"And she was the one leaving Ollie's that first day I came back?" Grey asked.

"Yeah, that's her," Eddie answered.

Trina hadn't run out of gossip yet. "Did you two hear what happened to Rae-Jean last night?"

"Rae-Jean Franklin?" Eddie asked, leaning his elbows on the tabletop.

Trina nodded and leaned closer to them. "Arrested for possession of meth."

Grey felt as if someone had just coldcocked him. A buzz started in his ears.

"I hear that's nasty stuff," Eddie said.

Tuning back in, Grey realized that for a few moments he'd been far away, recalling inmates he'd known who started with meth and ended in prison. "Is that news for sure? About Rae-Jean, I mean?"

Trina nodded grimly. "Yeah, the little guy didn't want to go home to his mom. That's why he ran off and then he was afraid of what she'd do to him because he'd run away. That's why he let the searchers pass him by earlier that day."

"Heard he hid in a hollow tree trunk right where they were searching," Eddie added.

"That's right. He's afraid of Rae-Jean. It's terrible—a kid that scared of his own mom. You know they say that meth or crack or whatever you want to call it can make people violent, crazy."

"I heard she wasn't even home when they tried to find her the night her kid went missing," Eddie said.

"Right you are. Out partying with her supplier, they think. Anyway, Chaney's custody struggle with her over the kid is finished." Trina turned away and greeted another customer.

"Poor Rae-Jean," Grey murmured half to himself.

Eddie cocked an eye at Grey. "Poor Rae-Jean? What about poor Chaney and poor Young Jake?"

Grey shook his head. He couldn't explain to Eddie why his sympathy went first to Rae-Jean. Chaney would get custody of his son. Young Jake wouldn't have to go to the mother he'd come to fear. But Rae-Jean would have to face losing her child perhaps permanently, public humiliation, detox and maybe jail time. And for what? Getting high?

"Hey," Eddie interrupted Grey's ruminations. "You going huntin' this year?"

Grey grinned. Eddie was still the same old Eddie. "No, a felon stays clear of guns. But," he went on quickly, "I think what you're really asking is can you hunt on our property again this year. And yes, of course you can."

"As long as your aunt gets her usual cut of the venison?" Eddie grinned.

"Yep." Grey let his spine relax against the tall wooden booth back. How good it was to just relax with his oldest friend, easygoing, fun-loving Eddie.

Eddie started talking about his hunting exploits last year and Grey let himself simply enjoy being with someone he could relax with.

━━━

ON FRIDAY EVENING, Trish watched Grey drive up the gravel road to her trailer. Tom had called to ask that she and

Grey do a round of collecting food for the local pantry. She was all too aware that just a few yards away through the woods, her father might be looking out his windows. That he might recognize Elsie's sedan. Florence had called her and recounted to Trish her father's harsh words to Grey at the congregate meal.

Trish pushed this aside. Her father had a problem with Grey. She didn't. And she had things she must discuss with Grey even if he wouldn't welcome her broaching the topics. But bad things were happening, like the two recent hit-and-runs, and it was her job to stop them.

Elsie's Chrysler pulled up in front of Trish's trailer. Snagging her jacket, a new fleece one printed with a colorful pattern of fall leaves, she bounded down the metal steps to where Grey had parked. He started to get out to open the door for her but she climbed in without ceremony. She didn't want this to feel more like a date than it already did. If she knew anything about Grey by now, he wouldn't be happy about the two of them being a team for this errand. "Hi."

"Hi." Grey gave her a look that she recognized, had expected. He was going to try to shove her away. His next words proved her right. "Trish, you don't have to come with me. I can handle this by myself."

She had prepared her answer to this. Working together like this didn't need to have romantic overtones and she wasn't going to give in to Grey's phobia about being seen with her. "Tom said he wanted us to do this together." *Okay, Grey, let's see you weasel out of that one.* Her unspoken aside was flippant but she was having a hard time dealing with this man who seemed to push away any positive overtures of friendship. She understood why of course. But she didn't like it. And she wasn't going to be bound by it.

"Okay then," he said. He turned around and drove them out onto the road.

Trish pulled a folded piece of paper from her pocket. "I have the list of places where we're picking up food."

"Me, too."

"Guess Tom thought we both needed help." She grinned innocently.

Grey nodded and drove toward the first stop, a church outside of Winfield. They rode in silence. Trish couldn't decide whether to come straight out with what she was thinking. Would it help Grey open up or shut him down tighter than ever? *Who am I kidding, Lord? When have I ever left well enough alone?*

She plunged ahead, hoping that her honesty would help Grey talk out his feelings about the recent incidents and maybe she'd glean some insight about them, perhaps open a line of investigation that hadn't yet occurred to her. "What do you think of this second hit-and-run accident on Bear Paw?"

He sent her a sharp glance. "I don't know what to think," he muttered, then looked straight ahead.

"Somebody has it in for you."

"Who doesn't?"

"I don't. The sheriff, Andy, Chaney—none of us do." She shifted on the seat, angled toward him. "I can't see you taking some kind of twisted pleasure in repeating..." Her voice faltered.

"The crime that killed two people and sent me to prison."

So Grey wasn't afraid to confront the truth, either. "Who hates you enough to do this?"

"Do you want a list?" He slowed to let a doe and her fawn decide whether they were going to cross in front of him or retreat into the woods.

"My father's angry, but I don't think he's mad enough to take a chance on killing someone just to make a point." She hoped she was right.

"I didn't mean to implicate your father." Both deer, colored with the darker winter coat, finished strolling across the road. Grey started the Chrysler moving again.

"This must be getting to you," she said.

"Are you clairvoyant or something?" he asked drily.

She ignored his sarcasm; he had a right to it. "I wish. Then I'd know who did this. And if they intend to do it again. I just don't get it. Do you?"

"Get it?"

"Get why someone is doing this? I mean it won't have any effect on your early release unless you could be connected to the accidents. What's the motive?" She'd set it up and now she waited.

"Maybe just getting to me, making me squirm is enough."

She frowned. "Yeah, I guess someone might want that." Like my father. Like Hank Valliere. And his son, Lamar.

"Let's change the subject, okay?" he suggested with an edge to his voice.

Okay, on to hot topic number two. He really wasn't going to like this one. "Chaney wants to know what he can do to let you know how grateful he is for your—"

"He can get Bucky a new chew toy." Grey sounded disgusted. "Bucky was the one who heard the kid and went and found him. Frankly all I did was slow Bucky down."

"Don't push aside sincere gratitude. Perhaps we would have found Young Jake the next day with the state dogs. But by then, the little guy would have been in worse condition. His hypothermia was just mild and he'll suffer no ill effects from his twenty-four-hour-plus exposure."

Grey looked pained.

She'd had enough of this. "Okay, spit it out. What's sticking in your craw?"

Grey looked away from her and shook his head as if shooing away an annoying fly.

"Out with it."

He turned to her, suddenly looking and sounding fierce. "Finding Jake—I just did something anyone would do. Just like I did for Andy that first night. Just because I'm an ex-con, everyone acts like my showing common decency is some big deal."

Trish sat back, for once chastened. *I didn't look at it like this, Lord. How do I let him know that he's taking it all wrong? How can I break through, show him that to everyone but my father, he isn't an untouchable?*

She repeated the final word to herself. Then cautiously she reached out and rested a tentative hand on his sleeve. He tried to shake it off but she wouldn't let him. She tangled her fingers around the soft nappy flannel.

"You're taking it wrong," she murmured. "It's not that we expect bad behavior from you. You were never known to be a mean person, Grey. We're only trying to show you normal, honest gratitude. Really." She slid a bit closer, still not releasing his sleeve. "Don't push us away."

———

TRISH'S PERSISTENT touch broadsided Grey. He slowed the Chrysler as the church, their destination, loomed ahead. He pulled into the small gravel lot and parked. Then he closed his eyes, just letting the feel of her hand on his arm work its way through him, savoring it, memorizing it. He'd tried to ignore Trish but of course, he couldn't. She had a way of seeping over and around the shield he tried to put up between him and others.

Finally he opened his eyes. "Trish, I'm sorry if I've overreacted. Maybe you're right and I'm not reading this correctly. I just..."

"Just what?" she whispered, so close to him that he felt her breath on his face.

There was so much more he wanted to say. He wanted to say how good she looked in that jacket and how her smile brightened the gloom deep inside him. He couldn't, shouldn't say that. But there was something that he must say.

Whether she'd felt the same bond forming between them as he had. It couldn't be. "Trish, I just want to take care of Elsie until she doesn't need me anymore. And then I'll go away and start over where no one knows me. That's all."

Would she take his meaning? He expected her to pull away and let them get back to the business at hand.

She didn't move. She released his sleeve, but her hand rose instead of fell. He watched it rise slowly, almost mesmerized by it.

She touched his cheek.

Grey thought he might lose consciousness. Her soft hand upon his cheek was the most wonderful sensation he could ever recall experiencing. Almost without thinking, he turned his face full into her hand, craving more of this freely offered paradise.

She slid up onto her knees, leaned toward him. He nearly stopped breathing. Their mouths were only a fraction of an inch apart. She was gazing at his lips. He could almost feel her lips pressing against his. With his last bit of strength, he pulled his face from her hand. "We're here."

He saw her look of shock, of chagrin, of hurt. But he had to stop this right here, right now. Didn't he?

IN THE EVENING A FEW days after Young Jake had been found, he'd come back again to the shed behind the old hunting cabin. With his arms folded, he stood in front of the shed's open plank door. Over the past few years, he'd used Jake's old hunting cabin as a place he could go to get away from everybody. People were always in his face.

But ever since Sunday night when he'd seen the old woman and then found the sedan in here, he hadn't been able to get it out of his mind. Had the older woman really been Jake's widow, Harriet Franklin? The night he'd seen her or someone very like her here, acting so strange, was the same night that Young Jake had gone missing, and there'd been a second near miss at the same place on Bear Paw as the accident. What did it all mean?

He didn't like anything that reminded him of the accident seven years ago. He'd thought all that was behind him, behind everyone. And then Grey Lawson had come back to town. Stirring up all his bad feelings again.

He rubbed his forehead. He'd read today in the local weekly paper that the sheriff wanted people to be on the lookout for an older silver-toned sedan missing one hubcap. The sheriff had tried to trace the car by the make of the hubcap. But it wasn't conclusive unless he could match it to a car with the same hubcaps.

The exact make and year of a car couldn't always be discovered just by a hubcap. People lost hubcaps and replaced them with new or used sets and such. And there still was no conclusive evidence that the hubcap found at the scene had come from the car that had forced that guy off the road. It was just an active lead, according to the interview with Sheriff Harding.

He pulled the local newspaper article from his pocket. He'd torn it out earlier and now he edged around the large car in the small shed. He'd come to find out if this car was the one responsible for Sunday night's accident. He eased around the car in the tight quarters. He counted one, two, three hubcaps and then... One was missing. He examined one of the remaining hubcaps and yes, it fit the description of the one found at the scene of the most recent accident. He straightened up and rubbed his chin.

So now he knew what the woman, maybe Harriet Franklin, had been doing here the other night. She must be the one who'd been playing chicken. Who'd have suspected it to be Jake's widow? But more importantly, what was she up to with these two stunts? An old widow. Why would she want to run people off the road? It didn't make any sense.

Did she do it to make things hard on Grey Lawson? He couldn't blame her for that. He tested his idea and could find no objection. Would she dare do it again—now that the sheriff had one of her hubcaps? He pondered this. She might. Or she might not.

A plan began to form in his head. If she repeated her crimes, fine. If not, maybe he would take over for her. He wanted Grey Lawson out of Winfield just as much as she did. Maybe more. And if the games of chicken went on and things got too hot for him, Grey might break the conditions of his parole. Or decide that he and his aunt should move elsewhere. *Yeah, that's what would happen.*

His conscience twinged slightly. But he'd done what was right about Chaney's wife. He'd noticed over the past few months that she'd started hanging around bars most nights. And he'd kept his eye on her and he'd figured out what she had to hide. So he'd called in the tip that had sent the Ashford police to her house where they'd found meth. That would make up for whatever he did to force Grey out of Winfield. And besides, Grey shouldn't have come back here. He should have known nothing would go right for him here. And if he was too stupid to figure it out for himself, then someone should help him.

Chapter 6

I can't let anything like what happened between us on Friday happen again. On Monday afternoon, with this intention clearly in mind, Grey finally located an open parking place down the street from the town hall where the food pantry was storing contributions. Winfield streets were bursting with tourists in town for the fall apple festival. Today he was delivering the food he and Trish had collected on Friday. He sat in his car, unable to stop his mind from going over what had occurred when he and Trish were alone together in his car.

Once more he relived their near kiss. The memory of the gentle touch of Trish's soft palm made his cheek tingle. The urge to place his hand where she'd caressed him grew so strong that he gripped the bottom of the steering wheel to keep from giving in to it.

Why had she done it? What was she thinking? What if someone had seen them? What if her father had seen them? "I didn't see you slapping her hand away," his conscience jeered.

"It won't happen again," he growled. He'd make sure of that today.

Someone tapped on the window by his head. He jumped and then glared out at Florence.

"Sitting in your car talking to yourself—" she gave him a devilish grin "—will make people think you're a wacko."

He swallowed his chagrin, shook his head at her and climbed out of the Chrysler. "Hello, Florence. I thought you'd be taking care of Young Jake today." He'd heard through the grapevine that Florence had volunteered to take care of Young Jake when Chaney was out job hunting in the counties around Winfield. Walking around to the back of the Chrysler, he opened the trunk and lifted out two boxes of canned goods.

"Young Jake will be with me after school today. Chaney's gone to Washburn and Ashford to apply for jobs." Florence had followed Grey to the rear of the Chrysler and now she leaned over and lifted two lighter boxes full of cereal boxes and macaroni-and-cheese mixes. She set it on the pavement and slammed the trunk lid down. "One's a night-shift job cleaning at the high school." She picked up her boxes again. "That would be good for Chaney. He could sleep most of the day while Young Jake's at school."

"I hope he gets it," Grey said, walking beside the older woman up the street. Beyond them, the blue waters of Lake Superior glittered in the sunlight. Gulls screeched overhead. A ferry boat from Madeleine Island packed with tourists chugged toward a nearby dock. Grey was relieved that the games of chicken had halted and the tourist trade appeared to be unaffected, booming, in fact.

"If Chaney gets that night shift," Florence continued, "Young Jake will sleep most nights at my place." She entered the town hall door, which was propped open. A babble of voices floated up to them.

Grey shuffled down the steps behind her and followed her through the many other volunteers to an area stacked with boxes of food. Tom Robson—just the man Grey needed to talk to—met them there. "Hi, you two. Let me inventory what you've brought in." He held a clipboard in hand.

Under the glare of fluorescent lights, Grey and Florence set their boxes on a long institutional table and she took over and began telling Tom how many of each item, such as canned corn, green beans, chicken noodle soup, boxed cereal and macaroni-and-cheese mixes they'd brought in.

As Grey listened to this tallying and naming of items, he went over how he would approach Tom about Trish. Tom made up the list of food pantry volunteers. *All I have to do is ask Tom to put Trish with somebody else.*

But he needed to get Tom away from Florence so he could talk to him alone. He didn't think anyone else knew he'd been working alone with Trish last Friday. And he wanted it to stay that way. Unbidden came the memory of Trish rising to her knees, moving so close to him. He felt her warm breath on his face again.

He tightened his control and tried to make his mind give up the tempting memory. Why had Tom paired him and Trish together in the first place? It wasn't like Tom to miss the fact that Grey and Trish shouldn't be thrown together like this. Grey Lawson and Trish Franklin were the last two people in Winfield that should have been scheduled to work together. How had Tom totally missed something so obvious?

"Hi, are you Grey Lawson?" A stranger, a retirement-aged man with a direct gaze, had stopped at Grey's elbow.

Startled, Grey found it suddenly hurt to draw a deep breath. Dread pierced him like a needle between his shoulder blades. Who was this? What now? "Yes," he answered cautiously, "I'm Lawson."

"I was just having lunch at Trina's and she told me that you're available for handyman work and would be here today."

Two simultaneous reactions put Grey on hold for a beat or two. First, this was so unexpected. He'd been so distracted by recent events that he'd forgotten that Trina said she'd put out the word that he was looking for handyman jobs. And second, this just proved that his volunteering for the food pantry was common knowledge, which meant that his being paired with Trish was bound to get around, too. A disaster waiting to happen. He forced his mind off Trish and slowly let oxygen in.

"Yeah," Grey said belatedly. "Yeah, I can do small repairs, painting, yard work. What do you need?"

"My wife and I have a summer place out east of town along the lake. It's been six years since we last redecorated and my wife would like everything painted while we're away for the winter. Could you come over and give us an estimate sometime soon? We'd like to hire someone and then be able to relax and enjoy the rest of September. We always leave promptly for Florida on the fifth of October. Then you'd have all winter to get the painting and repairs done."

"You want me to do the work while you're away?" At this thought, Grey's stomach suddenly erupted with acid.

"Yes, *definitely* while we're away." The man grinned.

Better to get everything out in the open. Grey faced the man and told the gritty truth. "Did Trina tell you that I'm out of prison on parole?"

"Yes, she said you'd had a drinking problem in the past and that you had a tragic accident."

That was certainly putting it kindly. "Doesn't it bother you to have an ex-con working in your home?"

"Trina and several other people whom I've known here for many years vouched for you. They said you'd never had a problem with stealing or anything like that." The man paused to grin again. "And my wife and I don't have expensive antiques or art insured for millions. I'm a retired hardware store owner, not Mr. Got Rocks."

Grey allowed himself to relax, the tension easing out,

breath by breath. "Then I'd be happy to come out and give you an estimate. I'm free any day this week."

"How about tomorrow? Around nine o'clock." The man gave Grey his name, phone number, address and offered Grey his hand.

"Sure." Grey shook the man's hand, a good feeling flowing warm through him. *Thank you, God. Now I can help my aunt out with expenses.*

The man walked out. Grey turned and came face-to-face with Lamar Valliere. If looks could kill, Grey would have been lifeless on the floor. On his way past Grey, Lamar took pains to bump Grey's shoulder as hard as he could. Grey swallowed his reaction and turned away. His buoyant mood deflated.

Shirley Johnson was suddenly right in front of him. "Grey, we're so happy to see God working in your life."

This comment caught him off guard. But his first response was quick and silent. *Yeah, right. Tell that to the Vallieres, to Noah Franklin.*

"You've only been home a little over two weeks and God has given you two opportunities to show what kind of man you've become."

Grey felt his neck warming around his collar. "I was just there, that's all. I wish people wouldn't go on about it."

She leaned closer. "Well, I just hope some of this is getting through to Noah Franklin and Darleen's family. I've always known that Noah has never been himself since he lost his wife, but he just isn't making any sense—"

"Is my fiancée standing around gossiping?" Tom, appearing at Shirley's elbow, interrupted in a mock-serious tone.

Shirley stopped and turned around. "Got me. But I'm concerned about Noah—"

"Don't waste your time worrying about that old coot,"

Florence put in. "Come over here, bride-to-be. We need to talk to you about a bridal shower."

Grey glanced around the hubbub in the large room, wondering how he could get Tom away for the few private words he needed to say.

"I don't need a thing—" Shirley objected.

"I mean a bridal shower for Audra and the sheriff," Florence said, hooking Shirley's arm and pulling her away.

Grey and Tom were at last alone. "Tom," Grey spoke up before anyone else popped over. "I want you to let me—" The image of Trish hovering just millimeters from his lips shot through him like a lightning bolt. It made his voice stronger, rougher. "I'd like to do my rounds of picking up donations alone in the future. I didn't really need any help." Grey hoped Tom would just say okay and leave it.

Tom didn't leave it. "I put you with Trish for a reason, Grey."

Grey's mouth opened. He hadn't expected this reply. "What reason?"

"So people in this county would see that Christians forgive one another and that the lion can lie down with the lamb."

Grey's face twisted with irritation and disbelief. "What?"

"Trish's uncle was killed in your accident and she's a deputy and you're an ex-con, but you're both Christians and you both can work together for the good of others."

Another volunteer hurried up to them and needed to talk to Tom. Grey turned away, disgruntled. *Who said I wanted to be an example anyway, Tom? Don't I get a say in this?*

———

EARLY MONDAY EVENING, on the tenth day of October, Grey took a deep breath and opened the door to a church basement in Ashford. A condition of his early release was that he attend two Alcoholics Anonymous meetings per week for the first year. It hadn't been difficult to agree to this since he desperately needed to go to these meetings. In prison, the AA meetings were the only thing that had gotten him through going cold turkey from both nicotine and alcohol.

Inside, he followed a hand-printed sign that said AA with an arrow pointing to the right. He entered a small classroom, probably an adult Sunday school room, which smelled of disinfectant. It was stark with a long table and chairs and some other chairs around the edge of the room. He smelled the coffee that he'd come to expect and went to pour himself a foam cup of the bitter brew. He sat down in the nearest chair at the table. He always felt humbled, stripped in these meetings. Nowhere to run. Nowhere to hide.

A man who sat in the middle on one side of the long table cleared his throat and began to read the Serenity Prayer. "God, grant me the serenity to accept the things I cannot change; courage to change the things I can; and wisdom to know the difference."

Grey went over what he couldn't change in his life in Winfield. Noah Franklin and probably Hank and Lamar Valliere's opinions of him. In their eyes, he'd never be free of blame. He sent this frustration heavenward, releasing it one more time to God.

Then the man opened the Big Blue Book, the basic AA manual, and began slowly reading the Twelve Steps, pausing after each one as if giving them each time to recommit to these lifelines.

Number one was admitting they were powerless over alcohol, that their lives were unmanageable.

"Unmanageable" didn't really describe the horror of waking up in a hospital and hearing from Eddie in the next bed that by driving drunk he'd killed two people, two people who were better humans than he.

Number two was that a power greater than themselves could restore their sanity.

Yes, thank You, God. Then, unexpected, the image of Rae-Jean, frantic, bursting into the town hall weeping for her son, flashed in Grey's mind.

Number three was they had made a decision to turn their lives over to God.

That had been the beginning of healing for Grey, turning his eyes back toward God, the God his aunt had always loved.

Number four was that they'd made a searching and fearless moral inventory of themselves.

And I realized that my life had been aimless and destructive, finally fatal to two other humans. Then out of the blue, he thought of Rae-Jean again and Young Jake's pitiful plea. "I don't want a spanking."

Number five was admitting to God and to themselves and to another human being what they'd done wrong.

Confessing to God hadn't been as hard as telling another human being. After all, God knew everything anyway. But it had cost him to tell the truth to another prison inmate also in AA.

Number six was being entirely ready to have God remove all these defects.

After the accident, I was more than ready.

Number seven was humbly asking God to remove their shortcomings.

You're still working on that, aren't You, Lord? I'm sorry You don't have better clay to work with.

Number eight was making a list of all persons whom they had harmed and needed to make amends with.

Grey remembered this hard penance. He'd written letters of apology to Hank Valliere and his son, Lamar; Noah Franklin; Jake Franklin's widow; also Eddie, since he'd lost his girlfriend in the accident; and finally, Aunt Elsie.

Number nine was making direct amends with these people whenever possible unless doing so caused more injury.

Hank, Lamar, Noah, and Jake's widow had all sent his letters back unopened. Only Eddie and Aunt Elsie had accepted his regret.

Number ten was continuing to keep a personal inventory and when they did wrong, admitting it right away.

I'm trying to do this, Lord. I'm trying to stay straight, keep my head down.

Number eleven was seeking God through prayer and meditation to improve their knowledge of His will and His power to keep them.

Number twelve was trying to carry this message of spiritual awakening to alcoholics and to practice this daily.

Yes, Lord, help me as I adjust to freedom. Don't let me abuse it, fall off the wagon. I can't go back. I can't hurt Elsie again. Grey found himself gripping the flimsy foam cup and relaxed his hand before he crushed it.

The man who finished this reading closed the book and said, "I'm Bill. I'm an alcoholic." And then Bill recounted his story. It was like all the others Grey had heard at other meetings. Like everyone else's but individual all the same. Each one of them—under the influence of alcohol addiction—had wreaked havoc in their own lives and the lives of their families in unique yet similar ways.

Grey knew that he'd hear Bill's testimony and those of others repeated at each meeting. Soon he would know the stories of everyone who attended regularly and they would continue to be repeated over and over. When he was new to AA, this had bothered him. But he'd finally realized that this repetition emphasized that if he fell and went back to drinking, it would be the same old mistakes, the same old frantic despair.

Again, Chaney Franklin's wife, Rae-Jean, came to mind. He sipped his hot coffee and pictured her sitting alone in a cell in the county jail, shivering with eyes and nose running. She'd be deep in withdrawal now. More miserable than even he had been, giving up alcohol. Would they give her anything or just let her suffer?

The man finished speaking and Grey cleared his throat. "I'm Grey. I'm an alcoholic." And he told his story. All the while, Rae-Jean's tear-filled eyes lingered in his mind. What was this all about? *Rae-Jean isn't my problem, God. My plate is full.*

———

THAT SAME EVENING, Trish dropped by Chaney's log house to see how his second interview with the high school had gone and how he was adjusting to being a single dad. He'd looked really stressed yesterday at church.

Plus she was trying to keep busy to get Grey Lawson out of her mind. As far as she could, she'd stayed away from him since they'd done that one round of pickups together. She'd made a lame excuse last week, but in a few days, they would do another round of picking up donations for the food pantry. Whenever she was alone, she relived those few intense intimate moments they'd shared in that church parking lot. *Did I really almost kiss him? Am I out of my mind?*

She knocked on the door but heard Chaney's voice lift in anger. "You can't see her. She's in jail because she was taking drugs."

Her pulse speeding up, Trish entered the kitchen and hung her jacket on a peg by the door. She'd been right to come. "Hi, big brother. Hi, Young Jake."

The little boy burst into tears and ran to her. He wrapped his arms around her hips and buried his face into her waist. "I want to see my mama."

Chaney made a sound of angry frustration, a kind of loud hiss.

Trish held up her hand and pleaded with her eyes for him to keep silent. She hugged Young Jake and then ruffled his blond hair. "Hey, good buddy, why don't we go to your room and pick out a book and read it together?"

The little boy wiped his eyes and looked up at her. "Okay."

She took his small hand and led him to his upstairs bedroom and found a copy of "The Cat in the Hat." Soon sitting on his bed with an arm around him, she was reading the rollicking story to him. After that, she read "The Little Engine That Could." It was so cozy that she could almost forget the scene she'd walked in on downstairs. *God, help me find the words.*

Finally, she settled Jake on the bed alone with a story CD, in the bedside player and its read-along book in Jake's hand. "I'll go down and help your dad finish cooking supper," Trish said.

She walked into the kitchen and found Chaney sitting at the table. His expression told her he was drowning in his misery. The ingredients for spaghetti and meat sauce waited on the counter. A pot of steaming water for the pasta was coming to a simmer. She went over, turned on the other burner and began browning the raw ground beef already sitting in the skillet. She glanced over her shoulder. "How did the job interview go?"

"Don't know yet. I think it went okay." He paused to rub his face with his hands. "How did everything go wrong so fast? Last year at this time, Rae-Jean and I were fine. And now everything is broken, trashed."

"It's sad," Trish agreed. "But don't make it worse."

He looked up, his jaw hardened and jutted forward. "What do you mean by that?"

Trish needed to make him understand. But how? With a long-handled spoon, she moved the sizzling ground beef around the pan. It was going to be difficult to say this out loud. She'd never discussed her longtime process of trying to make sense of what had happened to her and her brothers all those years ago. And was still going on. "Do you remember when our mother died?"

"How could I forget that? And I was in my teens, you were only nine."

"I know. She died two days after my ninth birthday." That day would never be forgotten. She even recalled the way the afternoon sunlight had slanted in their kitchen window when Florence had hugged her and said, "Your mama is in heaven, Trish." Trish moved the spoon, turning the ground beef, suddenly mute with remembered grief.

"What's your point?"

She forced words over the swelling in her throat. "I finally realized years later that we not only lost our mother that day, we lost Daddy, too." She blinked away the moisture gathering in her eyes.

Only the sound of the cooking meat filled the kitchen. Searching for a distraction, Trish's mind went back to the feel of Grey's hard, lean arm under her fingers. She hadn't expected just touching his sleeve would exert such power over her. *I can't do anything like that again. He's on parole. I'm a deputy sheriff for goodness' sake.*

Finally, Chaney said, "I hadn't thought of it like that. But you're right. Dad's never been the same since she died. But what has that got to do with me and Rae-Jean?" he challenged her.

"Because Rae got into meth and abused Jake, she's facing jail time and all kinds of court-ordered penances due to the child abuse. Your little boy has for all intents and purposes lost his mother as much as we lost ours."

"She deserves it."

That's not for us to say, Chaney. But she merely replied, "Yes, you're right, but does Young Jake deserve to lose his mom to drugs and then lose his loving, fun dad, too?"

"He wants to go see her!" Chaney protested.

"If we could have gone to visit Mom, wouldn't we?"

"You're not making sense. She was dead." Chaney's tense voice still revealed his deep hurt, frustration.

"You're right, but..." Trish turned off the heat under the ground beef, drained it. She then opened the jar of spaghetti sauce, poured it over the meat and set the stove dial on simmer. The homey task calmed her. "Rae isn't dead but she'll probably lose any plea for custody. And her son still loves her and wants her. That's not going to change. Don't let this change you."

"I'm not changing," her brother muttered.

She turned to face him, leaning her back against the counter. *Lord, help me make him get this. It's too important to be misunderstood.* "From what I remember and understand now, when Mom died, our father must have sunk into a deep depression. I don't think he's ever come out of it. I think being miserable and ill-tempered has become a way of life for him."

"I think you're right."

The pot of water came to a rolling boil and Trish added the pasta and stirred it. Then she walked over to her brother and laid a hand on his broad shoulder. "Are you going to change into an angry, ill-tempered father or stay Jake's loving daddy? It's your choice, Chaney."

Chaney buried his face in both hands.

Trish could tell by the shaking of his shoulders that he was crying. She'd been raised with four brothers and knew he wouldn't want this noticed. Giving him a measure of privacy, she turned away and stirred the pasta and then the meat sauce —all the while praying.

Young Jake wandered into the kitchen. "The story is over." He sounded worn-out. "I'm hungry."

Trish smiled at him. "Supper's almost ready and I've invited myself."

"Come here, good buddy," Chaney said to his son.

Jake moved slowly over to his dad. "Don't cry, Daddy."

Chaney lifted Jake onto his lap. "Sometimes things hurt and even a big man, even a daddy has to cry. Don't worry, Jake. We're going to be okay together."

From the corner of her eye, Trish saw Jake chewing his lower lip. *Please, Chaney, don't get closed in by bitterness.*

"And don't worry," Chaney continued, his voice picking up strength, "I'll take you to see your mama as soon as they let us."

The little boy threw his arms around his dad's broad neck. Chaney hugged his son close and Trish rejoiced. Now if only she could reach her father. But that would take a miracle. A major miracle.

ON MONDAY EVENING, he eased onto the driver's seat of the musty-smelling gray sedan in the shed behind the hunting cabin. He felt around under the dash for the ignition wires. Fog, wonderful fog had begun gathering in the low areas just a few hours ago. It would be dark soon. Perfect conditions for his plan.

Two weeks had passed since the last of the two games of chicken. He'd hoped whoever was doing it would go on. Two incidents in two days and then nothing in two weeks. Someone had chickened out on him.

He torqued his body to one side and leaned down under the steering wheel. He had to hand it to whoever it was that had thought of playing chicken on Bear Paw Road in the first place. It was a perfect way to force Lawson to leave Winfield.

Every time he saw Grey it was like grit rubbing in his eye. It brought everything back as if the accident had just happened. It made him sick seeing Grey walking free.

Tonight, he'd take over playing chicken. He'd read all about the first two accidents in the paper and had decided he wouldn't do it at the same spot on Bear Paw. The sheriff might be watching that particular stretch of road.

Besides, he had a certain person in mind as a victim and knew just where this person would be driving. He had to make a point of whom he targeted tonight. In order for this third game of chicken to do the job, it had to put Grey under suspicion. Tonight was perfect because he also knew that Grey would be on the road alone tonight with no alibi.

Just last week, he'd heard through the grapevine that Grey always attended the AA meeting in Ashford on Monday and Friday nights. And on his way here to the shed tonight, he'd driven past Elsie's and made sure the Chrysler was gone.

But he'd be very careful how he did this. He didn't want to hurt the person. If all went the way he'd planned it, no one would get hurt except Grey Lawson.

Finally under the dash, he found the wires that he would soon use to hot-wire the car. His hands shook but he'd do this. He had to. He had to get Grey Lawson out of his face.

Chapter 7

The next evening Trish wore her new ivory slacks and a brown sweater the color of steeped orange pekoe tea that the saleslady in Hurley had said matched her eyes. She'd even swept her hair back on one side with a long rhinestone-encrusted tortoiseshell barrette that Andy's wife had given her for Christmas. She had dressed with care because she needed "armor" tonight as she went into the "arena." Or that's what it felt like.

Trish inched down step-by-step to the fellowship hall in the church basement, usually a welcoming place. But tonight was the bridal shower for Audra Blair, who was scheduled to marry Sheriff Carter Harding the Saturday before Thanksgiving. And any wedding shower seemed to bring out the matchmaking compulsion in all wives and widows. As an unmarried woman, Trish would be one of their "targets" tonight.

Cradling her gift in one arm, a French pastry cookbook, Trish paused on the lowest step. From below, the laughter of women and their high-pitched chatter enveloped her. Yet dissatisfaction filled her to the brim. Even if this had been a normal month, a bridal shower would have been a trial. But recent events, especially the visit she and the sheriff had made to Elsie's house last night after the third hit-and-run, had soured her. Attending a bridal shower was exactly what she was *not* in the mood for tonight. *But I have to stay. I work with Carter and this is for his bride.*

Grey suddenly appeared in front of her, eye to eye.

Her heart pounded like a blacksmith's beating hot metal. Sparks from the molten metal flickered through her nerves, drawing her toward him. "Grey," she whispered. The image from last night of Grey's face—darkened with shock and then anger—leaped into Trish's mind.

"Hi. I just dropped off my aunt," he muttered, skirting around her, and escaping up the stairs.

She gripped the railing, steadying herself. How could just seeing him affect her so?

"Trish, come on!" Florence hailed her from the open entryway to the fellowship hall. "I saved a chair for you!"

Trish walked into the brightly lit fellowship hall and let Sylvie Patterson, a fellow single woman, add her silver-and-white-beribboned gift to a table already piled high with presents. Trish leaned over and whispered, "Let me guess. We will be playing games first?"

Sylvie nodded. She and Sylvie, a tall platinum blonde who walked with a limp, shared a commiserating glance.

Before the opening of the presents and the cutting of the white sheet cake, Trish would indeed have to suffer through the bridal shower games. She'd rarely felt less like playing games in her life. Leaving Sylvie to preside over the gifts, Trish perched on the chair beside Florence. On her other side sat Uncle Jake's widow, her aunt Harriet. *Great.*

"I heard there was another game of chicken last night," Florence said, once again revealing her talent for saying just what Trish did not want to discuss. "That's the third, isn't it?"

Trish opened her mouth to give her reply, but was ignored.

"Whoever did it picked on Hank Valliere," Florence

plowed on. "I hear the nutcase nearly forced Hank off the road. What's up with the investigation?"

"All three of the incidents are being investigated," Trish mouthed in a colorless, resigned voice. She glanced around at the circle of women all sitting on folding chairs. Audra, a very pretty blonde dressed in pale blue, sat across from Trish. Her little girl, Evie, wore a matching outfit and in her exuberance bounced on her chair. *I don't want to discuss this now, Florence.*

"Does Grey have an alibi for this one, too?" Florence persisted. "I know Hank has been in Grey's face more than once and even in this very room not long ago."

Trish had heard of hearts sinking and now she knew what that felt like. Just before midnight last night, Trish and Carter had questioned Grey a third time about these incidents. Again, the image of Grey's hardening face flashed in her mind. Emotions swirled inside Trish, spinning too fast to identify. Only one longing resonated clearly—she yearned to wrap her arms around Grey and hold on tight.

I can't do that.

"I can't believe that Grey would do something so obviously stupid," Audra, the bride-to-be, commented a little louder than she needed to. "I'm sure Carter and his deputies will sort this all out soon." Sylvie was now passing around sheets of paper for the first game.

"And this isn't the time or place to talk about such things," Shirley scolded, taking one and passing the rest of the papers to Florence.

"Well, it looks fishy," Aunt Harriet piped up. "Who else has it in for Hank? I saw Hank confront Lawson right here in this room. Was Grey getting back at him for that? Or is Grey Lawson one of those sickos who goes around repeating their crimes?"

"Grey is not a sicko," Trish snapped before she could stop herself.

Aunt Harriet raised both thin, penciled eyebrows at her.

"My nephew has come home to take care of me," Elsie announced to the gathering. She sat across from Trish near Audra. She looked and sounded fierce. "And I don't appreciate whoever it is who's playing these nasty stunts. *Or* anyone who thinks that Grey would repeat the horrible accident that sent him to prison. Can't you see, Harriet Franklin, that someone's doing this out of spite?"

Silence.

Harriet flushed as red as her lipstick. "Who's doing it then if it isn't your nephew?" she demanded, but her lips trembled.

This has to stop now. "If we knew that," Trish declared in her professional law officer voice, "we wouldn't be discussing this. The sheriff would have arrested the person. Now let's not ruin Audra's shower." She sent her aunt a pointed look.

Harriet looked disgruntled but accepted the sheaf of paper from Trish, took one and passed on the rest.

Sylvie began to explain the game.

Trish stayed in her chair, hearing but not listening. *These dangerous stunts have to be stopped. And I must steer clear of Grey Lawson. I can't let him know that I can't get him out of my mind. I'm right in the middle of an investigation that appears to be in some twisted way connected to him.*

But of course, she was scheduled to go collect food for the pantry with Grey on her day off.

———

THE NEXT DAY, AFTER being patted down and searched, Grey entered the small interrogation room with Harold, a member of the local Narcotics Anonymous at his side. Grey hadn't been able to get Rae-Jean out of his mind. Memories of his own first lost days and weeks—after he'd left the hospital and faced jail, his body racked with withdrawal—made it impossible for him to ignore Rae-Jean. At Grey's request, Bill from AA had contacted NA and Harold had volunteered to come and try to help Rae-Jean. But he'd insisted that Grey accompany him. So Grey had called Sheriff Harding who had contacted the Winfield County Jail in Ashford. And here they were.

Grey and Harold eased down on the straight wooden chairs around the small, scarred square table in the absolutely plain room. Within a few minutes, the door opened and Rae-Jean, in an orange jumpsuit, shuffled in with a deputy gripping her arm. The deputy nudged her onto a wooden chair and handcuffed her to the chair arm. When he left, he closed and locked the door behind him.

Looking wilted and crushed, Rae-Jean gazed up into Grey's eyes. "I hear you found my boy." Then, in spite of clamping her eyes and lips shut, she began weeping.

Grey held back and let Harold move to the chair across from Rae-Jean. "Grey asked me to come and talk to you about Narcotics Anonymous. You've been having a rough time, I hear."

Rae-Jean nodded, still weeping. "I was so tired of working. I just wanted to have some fun. I didn't know it would turn out like this."

Harold began going over the material provided by NA. Grey rose and stood by the door, trying to melt into the background. Harold was nearly finished when the door opened and Trish appeared.

Grey stepped back as if she'd cursed him. His heart thudded. *Why is she everywhere I turn? Did she follow me here?* He noticed that Chaney and Young Jake were on either side of her. As the guard led them inside, Grey fell back from the door.

"Hello, Grey," Trish greeted him, not meeting his gaze. "When I called this morning to arrange for Chaney and Young Jake to visit Rae-Jean, they told me you'd be here with someone from NA. So I rode along with Chaney. We can leave here together in your car and get a jump on picking up those donations."

He nodded, unable to speak. What else could he do?

Young Jake pulled away from his father and ran to Rae-Jean. "Mama, Daddy brought me to see you!" He threw himself into his mother's arms.

Rae-Jean crushed him to her though hampered by the handcuff.

Before the guard relocked the door, Grey slipped outside and Trish followed him. They walked side by side following the guard out to the main area and then they were buzzed outside. The experience brought back bleak memories Grey was still trying to forget. He led her to the Chrysler where he opened the door for her and wondered how he could broach the fact that this would be the last time they'd make the food pantry rounds together. Grey didn't care what Tom thought about it.

Pausing there, she said, "I'm so glad it worked out this way."

What? He questioned her with a lifted eyebrow.

"Having the stranger from NA there will probably keep Chaney from venting his anger at Rae-Jean."

"We can only hope." Chaney hadn't appeared very pleased as he watched Young Jake with his mother.

———

TRISH READ MORE FROM Grey's expression than his words. *He isn't happy to have me pop up here.* She slipped inside the older sedan and hooked her seat belt. She knew what she had to accomplish today. She had to tell him that she couldn't do these rounds with him anymore.

Then why didn't you just call him and tell him that? Her conscience probed and found her weak point.

Because I wanted to see him again, be with him again, of course.
This hefty admission rumbled through her emotions, shaking
her. She never blinked in the face of truth. And she wouldn't
now. *I want him to hold me again like he did when we found Young Jake.*

She'd dated on and off through the years, but had never
formed a serious attachment to any man. Always, she'd
wondered when or if she'd ever find the man that made her
feel something more than mild interest. Now she'd met him.
Yet the man was so unsuitable that it boggled her mind.

"Why don't I just drive you home now?" Grey suggested,
backing out of the parking place. "We both know that this
pantry job doesn't really need both of us to do it."

He was making it easy for her. All she had to do is agree
with him. "No," her double-crossing lips pronounced.

"What? Why not?" Disbelief tinged his words as he headed
out of the parking lot toward the highway out of town.

She stared straight ahead, pondering his question. Why not
indeed? He'd put into words what she'd intended to voice. And
she'd contradicted him, contradicted herself really.

"Why not?" he repeated.

Trish closed her eyes, letting her attraction to this man roll
through her. His strength, his endurance drew her. She'd
witnessed him taking everything that her family dished out and
he still didn't give back evil for evil. Instead, for Noah's hate
and distrust, Grey returned love in finding Young Jake and now
by reaching out a compassionate hand toward Jake's mom.
Grey's feet were planted on solid ground, on the solid truth of
God's love.

Even more compelling, his masculinity made her feel fully a
woman—not a girl, not a tomboy.

"I don't want to care for you," she said low in her throat.
"But I do." Her words seemed to demand and occupy tangible
space and vibrate in the air between them.

There was a very long, active silence.

He accelerated on the highway. "I'm going to forget you said that. I don't have to tell you why. You know why."

His tone of dark resignation spurred irritation through her veins. "Why is this happening?" Her voice whipped out waspish, cutting.

"Nothing is happening."

His flat denial incensed her. She turned on her seat, facing him and gripped his red plaid sleeve. "Something is happening between us. It began that first night after we rushed Andy to the hospital. Don't deny it."

"I have to deny it."

"You aren't attracted to me then?" She tugged at his sleeve, more insistent.

"It doesn't matter. We both know why we can't..."

Everything that she'd concealed over the past month came flowing out. "Yes, I know every reason why we can't be together. I'm a deputy. You're a felon. My father hates you for what happened seven years ago. You're a suspect or may be the target in a case I'm investigating. But I've never felt like this about any other man. I can't just ignore that, Grey. It's not in me to ignore things."

When he didn't reply, she twisted the soft flannel of his sleeve tighter. "Don't stonewall. You feel it, too, don't you?"

"Yes." He spat the word out as if it tasted bad in his mouth.

"What are we going to do about it?"

"We're going to ignore it."

"What if we can't?" she whispered.

GREY STRUGGLED TO KEEP his reactions all inside, under cover. Why hadn't she just left well enough alone? Why had she spoken the words aloud? With everything that separated them, did it matter that he was drawn to her as he was to no other woman?

His determination hardened to marble. He'd drive her straight to her trailer, and then he'd do the rounds on his own in the future. From now on he'd make certain that he kept Trish at a distance. People who conspired to bring them together, such as Tom Robson, would be disappointed. *I am steering well clear of you from now on, Trish Franklin. You can bet on it.*

But as he drove, he found it impossible to ignore Trish's effect on him, just as it had been from that first night. Whenever he came within her presence, though they were deep in autumn, to him the summer sun broke through. She warmed the dark lonely places deep, deep inside him.

As he probed this feeling, a memory from his boyhood—before alcohol had dissolved his family—returned. He recalled playing outside for hours in the snow. He'd come inside and stripped off his wet socks for dry ones. And there was his mother at the stove, stirring hot chocolate for him that had heated him from the inside out.

When he was near this woman, her warmth radiated through him layer by layer but from within, like the hot cocoa. He'd tried to stop it. But it came despite him. It was happening now.

He glanced at her from the corner of his eye. Trish was staring down at her hands, lying open in her lap. He relived the enthralling softness of those hands, pressed against his face. Now her bright auburn waves had fallen forward and hid her face. He clenched his hands around the wheel to keep from brushing them aside so he could see her face, take in the velvety luster of her skin.

It was torture.

He pushed down on the gas pedal. He had to get her out of this car as fast as he could. How much longer could he resist her at this close range? Everything inside him clamored for him to park the car and draw her into his arms.

His cell phone rang. Without taking his eyes off the road, he plucked it from his shirt pocket and handed it to Trish. "Please do the talking for me."

———

TRISH OPENED THE CELL phone and pushed the green button. "Hello, this is Trish for Grey."

"Trish," Elsie's tremulous voice stuttered over the little silver phone, "tell Grey I need him. Tell him."

"Elsie, you don't sound good. Are you all right?"

"Need Grey."

"We'll be right there. We're less than five miles from your place. I'm going to hang up, and you dial 91 on your phone. Then wait. If you need help before we can get there, you'll just have to press the final 1. Okay, Elsie?"

"Yes. Come. Hurry."

"We'll be there ASAP!" Snapping the phone off, Trish turned to Grey. "Elsie needs us. She sounds faint."

Grey pressed the gas pedal to the floor and the big old engine roared down the highway toward Cross-cut Road. Trish didn't caution him not to speed, but just clutched the cell phone.

Within minutes they zoomed up the rutted drive and Trish raced behind Grey toward the house. Tethered outside the door and straining on his leash, Bucky was barking as if hurrying them on. Inside, Elsie sat slumped at the kitchen table, her head in one trembling hand. "I think it's my heart."

Grey scooped up his aunt and carried her out the door. Trish followed, shutting the door behind them. She ran ahead to open the back door for Elsie and then she climbed in beside her.

Behind the steering wheel, Grey barreled in reverse down the drive. Trish took Elsie's plump hand in hers. "Do you have pills or anything?"

"I took a nitro pill, but it didn't help. Can't seem to get my breath." Elsie panted and then closed her eyes. "Sorry. Didn't want to interrupt your food pantry rounds."

Wasn't that just like Elsie? Trish squeezed her hand. "We'll get the donations later. No problem." Trish cradled Elsie's cool hand in hers, remembering all the love Elsie, her favorite Sunday school teacher, had shown her after she'd lost her mother. *What would I have done without her, Lord? Please let this be a minor incident, nothing serious.*

Grey sped them to the Ashford ER in as good time as Trish could have in her police vehicle. He jumped out and rushed back with a wheelchair. Trish helped him settle Elsie in it and he pushed away toward the automatic doors. Trish parked the car. Then, upon entering the ER, she sank down on a stiff chair in the waiting area and prayed.

———

DARK HAD CREPT OVER the sky outside the automatic doors by the time Grey loped back down the hall toward Trish. She studied his face as he approached her. His large gray eyes claimed hers and she detected a flicker of—what? How could she describe it? It was as if he'd reached out to her in that moment. And then the look vanished.

"I'm sorry you've had to wait so long," he muttered.

She rose. "Is Elsie in a room?"

He nodded. "She's resting. She's going to stay overnight for observation. Her weak heart is acting up. I can take you home—"

"I could just call one of my brothers—"

"No, I have to go home to bring Bucky in and feed him

and then I'll come back with some things Elsie wants and spend the night here."

"May I see her before we go?"

"Sure." He led her toward the elevator. Silently, they stood side by side as it ascended to the third floor. Again, Trish felt Grey drawing her to him. But the doors opened and he waved her to precede him. "She's in 310."

Trish walked quietly down the hall to the door of 310. She peered in and saw Elsie, hooked to an IV. Grey hung back in the doorway while she hurried to the bed and gripped Elsie's free hand. "Hi."

Elsie opened her eyes and tried to smile. "Now don't you worry. I'm going to be fine."

"I know you will be." Trish leaned down and kissed Elsie's lined forehead. "You're too ornery to die."

Elsie rewarded this with a shallow chuckle and then wheezed, gasping out each word. "You see that Grey gets some food tonight. He doesn't eat if I don't make him."

"Don't worry. I'll make him something before I let him come back here. But I'm not the cook you are. Edible is all I can promise." Trish squeezed Elsie's cool hand. "Now you rest. We're going to feed Bucky and settle him inside for the night. Or I may take him home with me."

Elsie's eyelids slipped down as she nodded. Trish met Grey at the doorway. Without speaking, they left together.

———

WHEN THE CHRYSLER FINALLY turned onto Cross-cut off the highway, Grey said, "I'll drop you off at your place."

"I promised Elsie I'd make you something to eat."

"That's not necessary."

She turned and gave him a stubborn look. "We both have to eat. Why don't we stop and take care of Bucky and then go to my place? I have stir-fry in the freezer. Let's just cook that up quickly and then you can get back to Elsie."

He shrugged.

Every time she was alone with him, her sensitivity to Grey and his moods intensified. She sensed him folding in, completely shutting off communication. Elsie's heart episode had triggered this. Did he think Elsie might be dying? She recalled his previous statement about taking care of his aunt until she didn't need him and then he'd go somewhere and start over. Did he fear that this was happening sooner than he'd anticipated?

Grey leaving Winfield and never returning crimped her chafed emotions. And dread of losing Elsie made her want to sit in a corner and cry. She shook herself. *Don't get maudlin. Elsie will be fine.* But her words didn't convince her. Grey needed her now, needed her strong, not weepy and clinging.

Keeping this in mind when they arrived at Elsie's, she watched him feed Bucky and then got back into the car. They didn't exchange more than a word or two. His impenetrable silence brooded over them. They drove the few miles back toward her trailer and Grey parked in front of it.

He turned to her. Before he could dismiss her and drive away, she jumped out of the car, making off with the duffel he'd packed for Elsie. She rattled up her metal steps and unlocked the door. Her last glimpse showed her that Grey remained in the car, glowering at her trailer.

She stowed the duffel in her bedroom and then began to prepare a casual supper for them. In her compact kitchen she turned the local country-and-western station on low and lifted a skillet from a shelf. She opened the freezer and selected a bag of beef stir-fry and a package of boil-in-a-bag rice.

"That was clever, stealing my duffel," Grey said, looming in the doorway.

"Close that," she said, glancing toward him. "I can't afford to heat the great outdoors."

He didn't even respond with a trace of a grin. But he shut the door and sat down at the small built-in table, his back to her.

He was going to be a charming dinner companion, if she didn't shock him out of his dour mood. She cast around her mind and said the first words that came up. "I was so proud of you today."

His gaze swung to look into hers.

She poured a little olive oil into the skillet, and from the tap, she filled a deep saucepan with water and set it to come to a boil on one burner. It would only take a few minutes for the stir-fry. While she waited for the water to boil, she began to lay placemats and settings for two with her cheery yellow-and-white dishes—all as if Grey weren't watching her every move.

She wondered if he would finally crack and ask her what she'd meant, or would he ignore her? During the silence, the country station played the classic Patsy Cline song "Crazy" and the pot simmered gently.

"I didn't do anything today to be proud of," he muttered at last, staring down at his place setting.

"You didn't?" She went to gauge the progress of the water in her saucepan. Little bubbles were beading to the surface. Nearly ready. She opened the refrigerator and pulled out two bottles of water and placed them on the table. She opened hers and took a long cold swallow.

Grey untwisted the cap on his and followed suit. "I didn't do anything for Rae-Jean except bring someone from NA to talk to her."

Trish sat down across from him, aware that any wrong word or phrase could catapult him out the door without eating. And Elsie wanted him to be fed and Trish was going to do this small service for Elsie if she had to hog-tie him to the table leg.

She chose her words with care. "That was a lot. Not even

Rae-Jean's parents have been to visit her and they refused to put up bail so she could get out while awaiting trial."

"That's why she's still in jail?" Grey shook his head. "That's hard."

"Some people are hard. When my youngest brother, Mick, got caught at a drinking party when he was sixteen, my father wouldn't bail him out or get him a lawyer. Andy had to step in for our father and help Mick get through it."

"Mick shouldn't have been drinking at sixteen."

"No, he shouldn't have, but sixteen-year-old guys do things like that. It's called being young and stupid."

"Maybe your dad thought it would teach him more if he faced it alone."

"I wish that were true, but I think...I think that it's just that...that he doesn't really love us anymore." Trish was aware as these sad words flowed over her tongue that what she was finally saying aloud was what she had been thinking, hurting from a long time. She had never allowed the words to come to the surface before now.

Shaken, she pushed to her feet and went to the stove. She dropped the frozen rice bag into the boiling water and began stir-frying in the skillet.

Suddenly Grey was behind her. He switched off the skillet and with his hands on her shoulders turned her around. "Do you mean that? About your father?"

She looked up into his fierce eyes, one cold tear sliding down her face, betraying the truth. "Yes," she whispered, "I'm afraid I do."

His wonderful arms enfolded her. She rubbed her face into his flannel shirt. Such a hard chest under such soft fabric. Her brothers all overwhelmed her with their large frames and sheer bulk. Grey was tall but lean. His strength didn't take up so much space. She smiled at herself. What a silly thing to think.

"He should love you. Your father should love you." His

hand slipped up her nape and cupped the back of her head.

In the most natural response, she let him hold her head as she looked up at him. He bent his mouth and the glorious anticipation of his kiss sang through her nerves, awakening feelings she'd long ignored.

He kissed her and her senses erupted. He turned his head slightly and then he was kissing her again. She forgot every-thing but Grey's persuasive lips. And then he pulled his mouth from hers. She clutched his arms, unsteady on her feet.

"I shouldn't have done that." He eased from her and sat down with his back to her once again.

She struggled to bring her breathing back to normal. Turning on the skillet again, she swished the vegetables and beef around for a few more minutes. The aromas of beef, onion and oil floated upward. The words she'd spoken aloud about her father still left her feeling shaken. In Madison, she had made friends. And far from her father, she had been able to fool herself with the fiction that Noah just wasn't a touchy-feely dad. But ever since she'd come home, her father had frozen her out.

The timer dinged that the rice was done. She turned it off, poured the steaming white rice onto a platter and topped it with the stir-fry. She set it on the table between them. She bowed her head and asked the blessing. Then she offered Grey the serving spoon.

They ate in silence. Added to the awful truth she'd revealed was the kiss they'd just shared. For that moment, she hadn't been alone. But she couldn't look at Grey. If she did, she might put down her fork and lean over to initiate another kiss.

Kissing Grey had been all she'd anticipated. Now she'd admitted that she'd been anticipating the touch of his mouth on hers for a long time. How had he ended up comforting her when she'd wanted to comfort him?

The stir-fry disappeared, leaving the platter wiped clean.

"That was good." He unfolded his long lean frame from the bench. "Where's the duffel? I need to get back to Elsie."

She longed to move into his arms again and ask him to kiss and hold her. Feeling love radiate from him—if this was love—persisted. However, she honored his request and retrieved the duffel. "Don't worry about Bucky. I'll go over in the morning on the way to work to let him out and feed him. Okay?"

Wordlessly he handed her the key and walked to the door. With his hand on the knob, he faced her. "I won't say that I'm sorry I kissed you. But it can't happen again. You know that, right?"

She stared at him, her insides shriveling and drying up. "I'm not sorry, either, and yes, I know that."

He left.

She fled into her bedroom and fell facedown on her bed and wept. *Why did I have to fall in love with Grey Lawson, God? Is this a sick joke?*

———

HE SAT AT HIS TABLE and stared out at the darkness. His game of chicken on Monday, his attempt to push Grey out of Winfield hadn't worked. Grey had been questioned, but not charged. People around town had been sure it was Grey the first and even the second game of chicken on Bear Paw. But now people seemed to think it was someone who had it in for Grey. Which was exactly the truth. There had to be a way to turn this around. He had to think of a way to force the heat up on Grey. But how? He cast around for an idea.

He glanced down at the latest newspaper article about the third incident. Targeting Hank hadn't done the trick. Maybe he should pick on someone more important to the sheriff or someone that everyone thought well of. Maybe that would be enough to force Grey out of Winfield forever.

Chapter 8

Saturday morning, he'd chosen his next target. Coming to that decision made him feel strong again. He could pull it off. This morning, he'd parked down at the end of the street from his new target's house and business and started his new plan. He'd decided he'd go about this like the detectives on TV. First, they staked someone out, studied their habits and then set them up for the kill. Well, he wasn't going to kill anyone, but this would do the trick. He was certain of it. Then Audra Blair strolled out through the glossy green gate around her Victorian and down the street.

He frowned. There was only one problem with choosing her as a target.

JUST OFF THE HIGHWAY, Grey drove up to Chaney's black pickup at the mouth of the old logging road into the forest. Later he'd visit Elsie, who was still recovering from her heart episode in the hospital. After parking the Chrysler off the road, he got out and wondered again why Chaney had called him to come here. He'd only asked for Grey's help, told him what to bring and where to meet him. Was Chaney irritated at him for interfering with Rae-Jean?

Or had Chaney somehow heard rumors about Grey's supper with Trish in her trailer? Surely Trish wouldn't have told her brother about that. Had anyone seen his Chrysler there? Or had Chaney just listened to gossip connecting Grey and Trish?

Getting out of his pickup, Chaney walked toward him, his hand held out. Chaney, like Grey, had dressed for a hard workout on a clear fall morning.

Still uncertain, Grey shook Chaney's hand, and then let go. Keeping a healthy distance, he propped his hands on his hips. "So what do you need me to do?"

Red hair stuck out from under Chaney's ball cap, bright in the sunlight. Chaney rubbed his unshaven chin. He avoided a straight answer. "I've got my truck, my splitter and my come-along. I could do this alone, but it goes faster with two. Did you bring your chain saw?"

Grey nodded. *Why aren't you answering my question?*

"Then get it out and climb into the truck with me. We'll drive in as far as we can on this old road and see what we can find."

Grey returned to the Chrysler, opened the trunk and pulled out his battered chain saw. *Well, if Chaney called me out here to start something, I'm at least armed.* Soon, the two men in the pickup bounced over the uneven grass road. In years past, heavy-laden logging trucks had carved deep ruts into the sandy earth.

"Logging companies and some private individuals donated all this forested land to this forest conservancy so it could be kept in its natural state," Chaney said, pointing up one finger from the steering wheel. "But they let the food pantry volunteers harvest fallen trees for firewood for needy folks to heat their homes over the winter."

So that was it. *But why me?* Grey nodded, recalling something. "Aunt Elsie says she's been one the recipients of this wood." Guilt over being incarcerated for seven years and unable to help her sank sharp teeth into him. "She only has her social security to live on, you know," he muttered.

"Yeah, some winters are colder and heating costs..." Chaney lifted his shoulders.

"It's good work," Grey said, hoping that Chaney's reason for asking him for help had just been given in full. He hoped Chaney didn't have a secondary agenda. But something made Grey suspect there might be more to come.

Chaney glanced at him. "Good for the people. Good for the forest. Keeps it freer of fuel for forest fires. Here we are." Chaney parked the truck and they both got out and walked to the back of the pickup.

Chaney let down the tailgate of his truck and hefted out the come-along, a metal contraption that could be hooked onto a tree. With its help, they could drag a tree out to where it was accessible to be cut into fireplace or woodstove-sized logs. "We leave the softwoods. Just look for maple or oak, some fresh birch. Pine burns too fast and hot for home-heating, though I often put in some pine for kindling."

In a few minutes, Chaney and Grey dragged a fallen maple tree out into the clearing near the parked truck. Grey pulled the rip cord and started his chain saw roaring, slicing the tree into measured logs.

His eyes kept straying to Chaney's head of red hair, so like Trish's. Would Chaney have asked him to come if he knew that Grey had been kissing his sister just a few days ago? Memory of Trish's softness coiled through him. Grey's neck warmed.

Chaney began using the low-slung, bright red log splitter, which had been hitched behind his truck. Systematically he set each log in, then split it into halves and then into quarters. He hefted the firewood up into the bed of his truck; each armload landed with satisfying thuds.

Grey tried to focus on cutting the tree into logs. Working so closely with Chaney kept bringing Trish to mind. Why was it that the very person he shouldn't be thinking about was the one he couldn't get out of his mind?

The two of them finished the maple and then retrieved an oak. Grey reveled in the sheer exercise of it. Occasionally, in spite of the gasoline smell from their chain saws lingering in the air, he'd catch a whiff of the clean smell of the fresh-cut maple and oak and cedar and the piney scent from the surrounding forest and breathe in deeply.

As his muscles warmed, he shrugged out of his heavy sweatshirt. They dragged out a freshly fallen birch, which was still hard enough to burn and began working on it. In the middle of the pine-green, red-and-yellow maple and golden-oak forest, all his drab years behind bars dissolved in the clear autumn sunlight. Freedom felt good.

From out of nowhere, he was blindsided again with the sensory memory of holding Trish in his arms—as if one good feeling triggered the other. He'd tried to put a lock on that rich experience—the glory of kissing Trish—but it kept bobbing up of its own accord.

His disobedient lips tingled as if she were there with him, sharing more sweet kisses. *What am I some kind of idiot? Have I lost my mind completely?* He shook his head, making every effort to enjoy the task at hand and hoping to rid himself of the sensations set off by the mere memory of holding Trish...

⸻

CONTINUING HIS SURVEILLANCE, he followed Audra down the street toward a side street. The problem with Audra Blair as his target was that she didn't drive much. But she was the perfect one. Audra was the sheriff's fiancée and they were about to get married. When he ran her off the road, the sheriff would be on Grey's tail quickly. And everyone would be flapping their jaws to put Grey back behind bars.

He'd just have to be patient and keep staking her out. She'd have to drive out of town sometime soon and if she did on a foggy night, he'd be right behind her. He rubbed his sleep-deprived eyes. He never got a full night's sleep anymore. He kept dreaming of the day after the accident and he'd wake up thrashing in bed. It wasn't right. *I can do this. I will do this. I have to do this.*

GREY FINISHED THE LAST slice of the birch. He straightened and stretched his spine and muscles. He turned to find Chaney reaching into the space behind the driver's seat. From a cooler there, he pulled out two cans of soda pop and tossed one to Grey. "We've nearly got the truck full." Chaney sank down on the running board of the truck.

Grey lowered himself onto one of the logs he'd just cut, facing Chaney. Something about the way Chaney fidgeted and kept looking at Grey and then away, put him on alert. He sensed that Chaney did have something more to say. He prepared himself for whatever might come.

Chaney took a swig of cola and wiped his forehead with his sleeve. "I don't know about you, but I worked up a sweat."

Grey nodded. Was Chaney going to warn him away from Trish? Should he tell Chaney not to bother, that he was steering clear of her?

"That was hard the other day," Chaney said, looking past Grey's right ear into the heart of the forest.

A shadow from above moved over the high wild grass in front of Grey. He shaded his eyes and looked up. An eagle flew overhead, circling to find something to swoop down and eat for a midmorning snack. *What are you talking about Chaney?*

"I mean taking Young Jake to see Rae-Jean."

So that's what Chaney wanted to talk about. Grey's tension didn't ease. *What does he want from me?* "Your wife has gotten herself into a bad mess," Grey said in a neutral tone.

"I've been so angry with her." Now Chaney stared at the soda can, clutched in one hand. "We've been married nearly eight years and then a year ago, she just changed, you know what I mean?"

"No, what changed?" *And why are you asking me? What do I know about being married?*

"Well, we've been working on the log house for the past five years. I mean we saved a lot of money since we did most of the inside finishing ourselves. She always worked right along with me and seemed happy about what we were doing. Suddenly she was sick of the place and she stopped helping when I had stuff to do and the house was a mess all the time. I asked her what the matter was and she'd just give me these funny disgusted looks."

Completely out of his depth here, Grey wondered what to say to turn the discussion away from Chaney's ailing marriage. Young Jake needed his mom and Grey didn't want to say anything that might cut the boy's contact with his mother. But in a way, Young Jake needed to be protected from his mom. Grey looked skyward at the eagle, so far above all these problems. What would it be like to just fly away? "Do you think she was on drugs then?"

"I don't know. What do you think?"

Grey shrugged. "Maybe it doesn't matter. What matters is that your wife, the mother of your son, is in jail, facing drug and child abuse charges. What are you going to do?"

"That's the question, isn't it?" Chaney fell silent, sipping from his can and also watching the eagle circle above them.

Frogs at a nearby creek chirped and cicadas and crickets clicked and buzzed. The first hard frost was late in coming this year.

"I don't think I'm the one who has the answers," Grey finally said.

"But you brought that guy from Narcotics Anonymous to see Rae-Jean. Do you think that she'll be able to kick drugs?"

"No idea. Meth is a vicious addiction. It alters a person's brain. It's concocted of poisons. Everything depends on how much she wants to kick it."

"My boy still loves her." Chaney crushed the can under his heel.

"She's his mom. Kids don't hold grudges. They just want love regardless." With a stab of remembered pain, Grey recalled the day his mom had dropped him off at his aunt's and driven away—never to return.

Had his mother been on drugs as well as alcohol? He'd never figured out what happened. He didn't even know if either of his parents still lived or not. In the past, he'd tried to fill the emptiness of that reality with alcohol. It hadn't worked.

Grey rose to bring this uncomfortable discussion to a close. "Chaney, I will give you this advice." He handed the other man his empty can.

"What?"

"Don't try to keep your son from seeing her, but don't let her use Young Jake to get to you."

"What does that mean?" Chaney rose, too.

This Grey had learned the hard way. It had been easy to blame his alcohol abuse on his parents deserting him. But blame made nothing better, only worse. "Addicts are good at one thing—trying to make everyone think that their addiction is everyone else's fault, not theirs."

Chaney gave him a confused look.

"Always stay with Jake when he's with her and if she starts

making excuses for her behavior, point out the truth. Just the plain truth. Don't get mad or mean. Just speak the truth."

"In love?" Chaney finished the familiar Bible verse.

Grey nodded. *If you have any left for her.* "Let's get another tree and pile it on. We can drive back slowly and fill up my trunk with the logs from the last tree."

Chaney nodded and stowed the cans in the truck. He pulled his leather work gloves on and they walked back into the woods to harvest another tree.

As Grey trudged over the uneven ground, he relived the vivid memory of Trish's despairing voice when she'd told him she thought her father didn't love his children anymore. No wonder he'd kissed her. He wondered how it felt to have a father so close, but still feel unloved?

Grey's mom had left him at twelve, but before she'd left, she'd signed his guardianship over to her sister, Elsie. She'd cared enough to give him to someone who would love him. Did Chaney feel the same rejection from their father as Trish? Was Rae-Jean's love for her son strong enough to motivate her to give up drugs?

I hope so.

———

HE'D FOLLOWED AUDRA all morning and afternoon and now he had to go to work. She'd spent her whole day walking around town. She'd never gone near the car in Shirley's garage that she borrowed when she needed to drive somewhere. This was going to be harder than he'd thought. What if the next time she drove out of town there wasn't any fog? He had to have fog so no one would recognize him. And soon it would be too cold for fog. The earth would cool just like the winter wind, and fog would no longer rise in the evenings.

He drove away, his stomach bubbling with acid. He popped

two antacid tablets into his mouth and chewed. If he didn't have an ulcer already, this might give it to him. Why did everything have to go wrong all at once? It was like a plot against him.

———

JUST AFTER NOON ON TUESDAY, Grey helped Elsie into their house, finally home from the hospital. Bucky wagged his tail and woofed his hello. His aunt felt frailer to Grey; she'd lost weight. "Do you want to go to bed right away?" Guilt over his plans for this afternoon pinched him.

"No, I'm sick to death of lying in a bed. Let's get me settled into my recliner and I'll watch a little TV." Elsie leaned on his arm.

He helped her into the small neat living room and onto her ancient rust-colored recliner, adorned with crocheted antimacassars. He fetched the remote control for her.

"I remember the first time I saw one of these——" she waggled the remote at him "——I thought, how could anybody be so lazy that they couldn't even get up to change the TV channel." She chuckled. "I didn't know then how old bones can ache."

Nothing ever got Elsie down for long. Grey leaned over and kissed her forehead. "I'll put the kettle on for you."

"Thank you, dear." She patted his arm and then pressed the power button. A woman's voice came on, explaining how to prepare a garden for winter.

When a car drove up, Grey, in the kitchen again, twinged with guilt. Shirley Johnson opened the door and greeted him. Bucky trotted onto the kitchen linoleum, his toenails clicking. He let Shirley pet him and then Bucky hurried back to Elsie.

"Thanks for coming, Shirley," Grey said, pouring steaming

water into a teapot. "But maybe I should just stay home this afternoon."

"I'm here, Grey. Now don't fuss. That tea smells lovely and I brought a few samples of Audra's baked goods." Shirley waved a white paper bag.

"Elsie won't complain about that."

Shirley walked past him into the living room and he heard the women greeting one another.

Grey brought in the teapot and two mugs and set them on a nearby end table where Shirley could reach to serve both of them.

"Elsie, Shirley's going to spend the afternoon with you. I have to finish up a job for that guy on County N Road. He wants to check it out and pay me before he heads south for the winter. But if you'd rather I stayed—"

"I could stay by myself," Elsie objected.

"Grey didn't ask me to come," Shirley said. "I offered. Audra dropped me off. She's going shopping and then for another fitting of her wedding dress. She'll pick me up on her way home."

"I'll be home as early as I can," Grey promised, his hands in his back pockets.

Shirley nodded. "Good, because Tom and I need to be at the high school by seven-thirty this evening. Chad's chef for tonight's reception and showing off what the Everyday Living classes are doing."

"No problem." Grey hesitated to leave.

Shirley began to pour the tea. "It's been too long since we had a nice chat and some of Audra's goodies and I want to tell you all about the wedding plans."

"I think it's so sweet that you and Audra are having a double wedding," Elsie said, pushing the mute button. "I'm so anxious to hear all about it."

Grey relaxed. He wouldn't be missed. Laying a slip of

paper by Shirley with his cell phone number on it, he left the women to their conversation.

As he drove toward the job where he was laying quarry tile in a bath and entryway, he thought about Tom and Carter, who'd both found the perfect women for them. He halted his mind just as it was trying to take him back to Trish's kitchen. *It's over. Period.*

HEADING HOME FOR ANOTHER solitary night, Trish stared out her sheriff's Jeep window. She'd borrowed the Jeep since her SUV was again in for some bodywork. She dreaded going home. Ever since the evening she'd kissed Grey and confessed her deepest fear, her trailer had not been a refuge, but an empty, very lonely space. Tonight, heavy mist had gathered in the low spots and already had billowed to the treetops. Another perfect night for a game of chicken—a pleasant thought. A week had passed since the last such event. Would the maniac responsible for the first three be out tonight? Her cell phone rang and she picked it up.

Shirley Johnson's voice came over the phone. "Trish, sorry to bother you, but can you do me a favor?"

"I'm on my way home, Shirley. What do you need?"

"That's what I thought. I'm with Elsie at her place. Grey brought her home from the hospital today and I've spent the afternoon with her. But Audra will be picking me up anytime now and Grey has been delayed. Can you come and sit with Elsie until he gets home?"

In the background, Trish heard Elsie's muffled protest and Shirley's response. Trish had avoided Grey for days. Now this. *Shirley, you don't know what you're asking me. B*ut of course there was only one answer Trish could give. "Sure. It's on my way. I'll head there right now."

"Thanks." Shirley hung up.

Trish made a U-turn and headed south toward Cross-cut. She hit a contact number on her cell phone. The fog draped around her like an opaque veil. Trish slowed so she wasn't outpacing her visibility.

After three rings, Grey's voice came over the line. Just the sound of his deep hello tightened her nerves and melted her reserve. She took a firm hold on herself. "Grey." She nearly barked the words, trying to sound impersonal. "Shirley just called and asked me to stay with Elsie till you got home. I'm on my way."

He made a sound of frustration. "No, I'll leave this job now—"

"No, get your job done," she interrupted him. *Don't overreact, Grey.* "Just call me at Elsie's when you're about to leave and I'll head home then. Okay?"

Silence over the line. Finally, Grey said gruffly, "Okay."

She hung up without saying goodbye. Her backstabbing memory brought up Grey's lush haunting kiss. She understood completely why they could not let their attraction go any further, but that didn't make it any easier.

She turned onto Cross-cut. The thick fog worried Trish. *Dear Lord, don't let anything bad happen tonight.*

Suddenly red taillights flashed in front of Trish's Jeep. The rear revealed to her an older gray sedan. She gawked. Under cover of the fog, had the sedan just now come out of one of the many private side roads? Or had it been there all along just beyond her headlights, shrouded in the fog? But most important—could this be *the* gray sedan?

On alert, Trish hung back. Had the other driver seen her headlights and that this was a sheriff's Jeep? Separated again and invisible in the fog, she listened to the other vehicle. The sedan's engine rumbled rough and loud and she knew she hadn't heard it before. *It must have just been waiting to pull onto the road. But for what? Who? Why?*

Trish almost turned on her flashing lights. But she pulled back her hand. If this were *the* gray sedan, she had to catch its driver in the act to prove that he was the one playing the games of chicken. This might be the guilty sedan or it might just be an innocent driver.

She could still hear the older noisy engine ahead. She maintained her speed, but stayed back enough so her sheriff's vehicle wouldn't be seen. *She* could use the fog for cover, too. Then she heard the gray sedan's large motor roar forward. She pressed down on the accelerator.

Through the mist, the sedan's red taillights again shone brightly. The sedan had moved into the center of the road. She could see the bright yellow lines sliding like a broken ribbon under the center of the rear of the sedan. This was it—a game of chicken! Trish switched on her lights and siren.

Farther ahead in the impenetrable fog, a car horn blasted a frantic staccato. A squeal of brakes and tires on wet pavement. Then the crunch of an impact.

Trish's Jeep roared forward. She glimpsed the red taillights of the sedan ahead. The sedan accelerated, too. In a flash from the corner of her eye, Trish caught the sight of the other vehicle off the road. Just its taillights were visible.

Torn between pursuit and giving aid to the victim, Trish flipped on her radio and hailed dispatch. "I'm in pursuit heading west on Cross-cut Road. I need backup. And there may be an injured victim." She snapped off.

Keeping the rear lights in view, she accelerated some more. This must be it! Her heart pounded. She pressed harder on the gas pedal, trying to get close enough to see the gray sedan, its license number, its driver. The rough-sounding motor started misfiring. She sped up, tailgating the sedan. No license plate.

The sedan began to weave all over the road—back and

forth. Trish wanted to catch him, not have an accident. But she couldn't let him out of her sight. The sedan sped up some more. Then it slammed on its brakes, fishtailing on the wet pavement, spinning out of control toward the ditch. Trish swerved to miss it, and overshot it. Then she hit her brakes.

When she'd slowed enough to maneuver, she did a U-turn and went back for the sedan. The road was empty. She crept along through the murkiness, staring at the side of the road she'd seen the sedan swerving toward. She saw it then—a private lane overgrown and obviously rarely used. There were fresh tire tracks in the tall damp wild grass. She halted and called dispatch again.

This time Sheriff Harding came on the line. She quickly told him the whereabouts of the private road and that she was going back to the victim. "Right. We'll call the EMTs," the sheriff said. "I'll be out ASAP. I'm having every deputy called in to search that area." He hung up.

After getting out and marking the entrance of the lane with a red flare, she sped down the road back to the car off the shoulder. She pulled in beside it, her blue lights rotating. She ran and opened the driver's side door. The airbags had deployed. Audra Blair moaned, "I'm hurt."

AS GREY TURNED ONTO CROSS-CUT, he heard police sirens. He pulled off the road. One sheriff's Jeep and then another flew past him, disappearing into the mist. Shaken, Grey pulled back onto the road and drove in the same direction. Just the sound of a police siren stripped him of his fragile confidence. What was happening that was so desperate that two police vehicles were hurtling down this quiet country road? And then the significance of the fog hit him. Another game of chicken?

Panic flashed inside him like an instant ice storm. *I'm on the road alone and some nutcase may have played another game of chicken.*

Grey literally didn't know what to do. His heart pounded. Nausea hit. *I don't have an alibi.* The fear of being hurled back into a prison cell tightened around his lungs. He pulled off to the side of the road, fighting to master himself. *I can't give in to panic. I've done nothing wrong.*

He forced himself to fill his lungs with air. He recited the Lord's Prayer and the Twenty-third Psalm and then prayed. Then he eased back onto the road and drove toward home. On the way, he passed a red flare sputtering brightly. He glimpsed still another police car turning in to the grassy lane beside the flare. Had the sheriff called out his whole force?

Farther on, he reached the flashing of blue police lights. A car was off on the shoulder. He stopped and pulled off the road and parked. His nerves had not improved much. Everything within him blared a warning.

But there was no sense trying to slink off home. He'd added two and two and they equaled a fourth game of chicken. And after each game of chicken, the sheriff and Trish had come calling at his door. Swallowing down the nausea, he got out and approached the vehicles. "Is anyone hurt?" he called out through the cloaking fog.

Trish appeared out of the mist. "It's Audra Blair. She's not bad. She was run off the road and her airbags were set off. She's just a bit bruised." Trish looked up into his face, her warm brown eyes overflowing with worry. "Why didn't you call me?"

She was worried about him. He shoved his hands into his jeans pockets to keep from reaching for her. "I tried but your line was busy."

"That fits. I had to call dispatch twice." She took another step toward him.

He stayed where he was. "I was just about to call again

when I was passed by police cars with their sirens on. Is this...is this another game of chicken?"

"Fraid so."

His fight-or-flight response surged into the danger zone. Adrenaline swamped him. He shoved his hands deeper into his pockets, keeping his reaction under cover. *I can't look guilty. And I can't show any obvious concern for Trish. She's here as a cop.* Elsie's home waiting for me and Shirley needs to go to the high school."

"I know," Audra said, walking forward on Carter's arm, out of the mist. "I need to pick up Shirley."

"You're going to the hospital to be checked for internal injuries," Carter insisted. "I'll call Tom to come and pick Shirley up."

"I don't want my aunt alone," Grey spoke up. No one was going to worry his aunt back into the hospital. "I brought her home from the hospital today. Am I free to go?"

"Where were you just now?" Carter asked.

"I just finished a job on County N. The homeowner came around twenty minutes ago and inspected the work and wrote me a check." Grey pulled it out of his wallet from his back pocket. "He locked up and then I started home."

"I was on my way to stay with Elsie until Grey got there," Trish added. "So Shirley could leave when Audra arrived. I was just on the phone with Grey."

Grey kept his eyes on the sheriff, who was holding his fiancée close. Resisting the same protective urge, Grey folded his arms that persisted in wanting to reach for Trish.

"So I guess some people could think I'm the culprit," Grey said, "but I wasn't." He couldn't prevent his voice from rising with his final words. "I just want this over, to be left alone."

"Go on home then," Carter said, nodding. "Audra, you'll sit in my car and wait for the EMTs to come and take you to

Ashford ER. Trish, I've called in everyone to search the area where the sedan left the road. I want you to head there now."

Trish agreed.

Concern for Elsie held Grey here. "I don't want you coming to my aunt's house around midnight like you've done the last three times—"

"I won't." Carter walked away. "I already have your statement and Trish's. Now go home."

Grey turned to obey and then turned back. "Have you called the Ashford ambulance yet?"

"Just about to," Carter said, halting.

"Why don't you let me take Audra to my aunt's house and have them pick her up there?" Grey offered. "She'll be more comfortable and you won't have to stay here with her." *What did I say that for?* Grey nearly kicked himself for offering this.

"Yes," Audra agreed, "I'll wait at Elsie's. I want to get out of this dampness." She shivered.

To Grey's dismay, Carter agreed and walked Audra to Elsie's Chrysler and helped her inside. "Take care of her," he said to Grey. Then before Grey could start his engine, Carter opened his ringing cell phone. He listened to the conversation. Grey, Trish and Audra all waited. Carter snapped the phone shut. "Dispatch got an anonymous phone call."

Chapter 9

Driving up the private lane to her uncle Jake's old hunting cabin, Trish still couldn't believe what the anonymous caller had told dispatch. "It just can't be true," she muttered to herself one more time. But reality kept poking its sharp beak into her face. The reality of the sheriff's red taillights leading her through the thick fog, parking and getting out into the damp mist which sprinkled her face like dew, treading the uneven ground near the old hunting cabin she knew so well. All were impossible to consign to the realm of fantasy.

Without a word, she followed Carter to the shed. Now they would learn whether the anonymous caller had lied or told the truth. Other deputies, some on duty and some called in, had parked their cars so that their headlights illuminated the shed. They all waited around the still-closed door. Trish felt her heart and lungs seizing up, jolting as if they were going to come up her throat. *Please, dear Lord, don't let it be true.*

In the semicircle of silent officers, Carter went forward and unlatched the plank door. He opened it wide. In the eerie headlight radiance, a gray sedan sat before them.

A kind of explosive mutter rippled through the deputies.

Trish gagged, speechless. The anonymous caller had been telling the truth. Was the nutcase playing dangerous games her own aunt Harriet? White-haired, plump Aunt Harriet was running people off the road? "I can't believe it," she said aloud. "I can't believe it."

"Don't jump to any conclusions," Carter cautioned. "The anonymous caller was male. Someone may have been using the sedan without your aunt knowing anything about it."

"That's true," Trish murmured, still feeling as if she—instead of Alice—had free-fallen down a rabbit hole.

"Okay." The sheriff turned to his deputies. "Those of you who aren't on duty can go home now. We don't have to do the kind of sweeping search I thought we were in for. But I'm going to stay and personally conduct this investigation myself."

"What about Audra and Evie?" Trish asked, trying to keep in touch with all of the realities.

Carter looked conflicted, his brows drew together and he grimaced. "Audra and Evie's with Shirley. I'm sure Shirley will go with Audra to the ER to be checked out. I'll call and if it's more than bruises, I'll go. But really I can do more here, find evidence that might prevent others from suffering accidents. Audra didn't appear to be in real distress—just shook up. And my future wife's no weakling."

Trish followed the sheriff's line of thinking but knew he'd still rather be with Audra. She didn't mention it, however. This crime scene might actually provide them with the identity of the criminal. The off-duty deputies melted away into the fog, returning to their vehicles and driving away. They took most of the light with them. The on-duty deputies had gone to their cars and had already returned with their crime scene kits.

"I'm staying," Trish said and started toward her Jeep to get her gloves and evidence kit and catch up.

"No," Carter said. "No."

She halted, turning to face him in the remaining light. "What?"

"No, you can't work this crime scene." Carter faced her fully with his hands propped on his hips.

"What?" Her mind refused to accept his words. "Why not?"

"Because you may be related to the person who's been doing this. I can't have a family member of the sedan owner on the investigation. Might lead to possibly being accused of tampering with the evidence."

Trish gawked at the sheriff, her tight throat unable to swallow. Dread filling her every pore.

"And your family could have a negative reaction toward you if we find out that your aunt is involved. They could view you as a traitor."

Trish stared at him, denial repressed low in her constricted throat.

"I want you to go home and tell no one what has happened tonight."

Trish struggled to quell the writhing inside her. *I have to stay. I have to find out who's doing this.*

Just then, a horn blared.

Both Trish and the sheriff turned toward it. Before Trish could see it through the fog's gray veil, she heard the familiar rattle of her father's truck. Within moments, her father emerged from the mist, marching toward her and the sheriff. "This is private property!" he shouted. "It's posted No Trespassing!"

"Dad," Trish called out. "It's me and the sheriff."

Her father pulled up short. "What? I was just driving by and saw all this light... What's going on here?"

"I can't tell you that, Mr. Franklin," Carter replied. "I must ask you to leave this area and not to mention our being here to anyone."

"Not tell anyone?" Noah came abreast of her and Carter. "What's going on?"

"I can't tell you," Carter answered again, "but I'm here investigating a crime."

"What crime?"

"Mr. Franklin—" Carter's voice was firm "—please leave this area and go home. I am not at liberty to discuss this investigation with you."

Noah glared at her. "What's going on, Trish?"

"Deputy Franklin," Carter said in a commanding tone, "is not at liberty to give you that information. Now I must ask you to leave."

"No one's making me leave until I'm ready to go," Noah snapped.

Carter called one of the other remaining deputies. "Please see that Mr. Franklin gets into his vehicle and leaves this area."

Her father sputtered with indignation. The other deputy approached him. At the last possible moment, Noah whipped away toward his truck, bellowing curses at the sheriff and her. The old truck rattled away, leaving a backwash of ill feelings.

"Sorry about that," Trish muttered, hurrying, escaping to her vehicle. Her father was unraveling. Just a month ago, he'd never used such language. It made her sick to hear curses from his lips. All this just because of Grey's parole? Was there something about her father she didn't know?

"Trish," Carter called after her. "Write up a report on what you observed on the road tonight as soon as possible."

"Right." She drove away, holding back hot tears of shame and frustration. *Was my father really just driving by Jake's property? Could he have been the anonymous caller? Or the driver who'd run Audra off the road?*

Driving through the fog, Trish tried to follow Carter's order and head home. But the thought of going to that silent, empty trailer filled her with unbearable loneliness that sucked out strength and hope. Also the very real possibility that her father would lie in wait at her house to question her made it impossible for her to go home. *But where can I go?*

Only one place came to mind—Elsie's cozy little log cabin. *I can't go there.* But she didn't want to go to her brothers and worry them about their father. She knew they didn't possess what she hungered for. Where else could she turn?

Even though the fog made it dangerous, Trish pulled off on the shoulder of Bear Paw Road. She gripped the steering wheel, trying to force herself to go home and just refuse to respond to her father. But what had he been doing near the hunting cabin? Her mind repeated her worries. Was he the driver? Was he the anonymous caller? *I can't face him. I can't face that.*

She bent her forehead against the center of the steering wheel. Never had an investigation weighed her down like this one.

Her spirit reached out, seeking comfort and strength. "Come unto me you who are heavy-laden and I will give you rest." The verse and others brought solace and strength as she played through her mind the memories of once again sitting in Elsie Ryerson's Sunday school class as a little girl, reciting memorized verses for hugs and candy.

New energy flowed through her, lifting her like a leaf on the wind. She straightened up. *Lord, I know Grey isn't the person responsible. And I can't go home. So if this is a big mistake in judgment, I'm sorry. But I have nowhere else to go, nowhere else I want to be.*

Before she let all the reasons why she shouldn't go to Grey win out, she'd eased back onto the foggy road and covered the few miles to Elsie's. She parked her Jeep outside the door and got out. She nearly ran to the door, startling two deer at Elsie's backyard feeder. They leaped into the surrounding forest. Before anyone could answer her knock, she let herself into the warm bright kitchen. Her pulse thrummed at her temples.

Bucky barked once and padded into the kitchen to her side. She stroked his soft ears.

Grey stood at the stove, stirring something fragrantly appetizing in a saucepan. Bucky left them alone.

Trish approached Grey, suddenly afraid that he'd push her away. Would he? But she couldn't deny her attraction to him. *I need you, Grey.*

"Trish, what—" he began.

With a daring she hadn't known she possessed, she rested her head on his chest and wrapped her arms around him. "Hold me," she whispered, implored.

For a moment, he didn't move.

Please, Grey, don't turn me away. She waited for his decision, not breathing.

Then he put down the spoon and his sturdy arms came around her.

Relief sighed through her. Grey's arms held all she desperately needed right now. She pressed her face into the soft knit of his shirt. "Just hold me." *I don't have anyone else on earth I want to turn to but you.*

Grey tightened his arms around her and his cheek brushed her hair. She let the comfort of his embrace work through her flimsy defenses, reaching deep within her heart to her soul.

A few minutes later, Elsie called from the living room. "Who's come?"

"It's me—" Trish turned her face so she could be heard "—Trish."

"Oh, my, I'm getting all kinds of company today. Shirley, Audra, Tom and now you."

"I hope we're not wearing you out," Trish replied, cheered as always by Elsie's welcome. Then she looked up into Grey's face and mouthed, "Did you tell her about the anonymous call?"

Grey shook his head.

"Don't," Trish whispered and Grey squeezed her to show agreement. She reveled in his touch and tightened her arms around his solid chest.

Elsie continued, "Audra was in a slight accident so Shirley went with her to the ER. Tom went to the school for that thing for Chad. I don't know what's going on in this town anymore. It's just one thing after the other."

Trish couldn't have agreed more. Though her father had directed his spiteful words at the sheriff, they'd stabbed her, making her recoil. Would she be able to stay in Winfield? A kind of panic unfurled—where would all this end for her father? A nervous breakdown? She looked up at Grey and mouthed, "Please kiss me."

He hesitated and then bent his mouth slowly. At last, his lips met hers. Oh, the blessed comfort of his kiss. Trish drowned in its healing balm. She could bear whatever might come now, survive anything.

But her conscience mocked her. *Are you forgetting what you are, who you are? This will never work between you and a felon.*

FEELING AS HAZY AND wispy as last night's mist, Trish walked between Carter and another young deputy, Josh, up the path to her aunt's house. Carter had told Trish that he and Josh would handle the questioning, but he'd wanted her along to hopefully ease her aunt's discomfort.

It was just after six o'clock in the morning. Aunt Harriet, who'd never had children, lived in the snug red brick bungalow on a side street in Winfield, the house Uncle Jake had built for them by himself in the 1950s. In the past, Trish had always looked forward to walking through Aunt Harriet's door.

That had changed with Uncle Jake's death. It had soured

her aunt toward everyone and everything in life. And now this. What would her aunt's response be today?

Up three steps to the side door, a sleep-deprived Carter walked beside her and he was the one who knocked on the white door. Then Trish suppressed a yawn from her own restless night, spent tossing and turning, waking every hour or so to check her bedside clock. Her small trailer had felt like a prison cell.

Then she noticed that her father's truck was parked back on the alley behind Aunt Harriet's. Her already low spirits slid to her toes. *Oh, no.*

Before Trish could point this out, the door opened and her aunt faced them. "Hello." Harriet's voice shook.

Trish analyzed the tone. Did she sound guilty? *Unfortunately, yes.*

"May we come in?" Carter asked. "We have something pressing we need to discuss with you."

Dressed in a dark blue polyester dress but without her usual red lipstick, Harriet nodded and stepped back to let them in.

At the sheriff's nod, Trish entered first, followed by Josh. Aunt Harriet looked guilty, but guilty of what?

Once through the tiny side porch, they were standing in her chrome-and-white 1950s kitchen. Unshaven and scowling, Noah sat at the table, drinking coffee. Harriet sat back down at a right angle to him. Trish and Josh leaned against the kitchen counter. Carter had asked her to come for her aunt's sake. But Noah's presence might make her presence a liability.

"I beat you here, Sheriff," Noah sneered. "I've warned Harriet just what you'd be coming for."

"And what is that?" Carter asked politely.

"To pin these nasty games on her instead of that Lawson. That's why you were out on her property last night with her shed open, right?" Her father's eyes were alight with malevolence. It chilled Trish like an icicle up her spine.

"I don't pin things on people," Carter said in a stiff tone that Trish recognized as dangerous. Her father had definitely put himself on the wrong side of the sheriff. But that seemed to be her father's intention—to set as many people as possible against him. He appeared to revel in being at odds with everyone.

"Just as I did last night," Carter said. "I must ask you to leave, Mr. Franklin."

"I'm not going anywhere." Her father grinned with malice.

"Then I'll have to take Mrs. Franklin in for questioning. I thought it would be preferable to take her statement here in the privacy of her own home. But if you refuse to leave, I have no alternative."

Trish dreaded her father's reply to this challenge.

Noah ignored the sheriff. "Harriet, you don't have to answer any questions. I'd get a lawyer—"

"Mrs. Franklin, let's go," the sheriff said. "Get your coat, please. If you want a lawyer to be present while I question you, you may phone one from the station—"

"You can't just take her without a warrant," Noah blustered, rising from his chair.

Her father was digging his hole deeper and deeper. Trish took in a barbed breath.

"As a matter of fact, I can," the sheriff said. "I can question anyone I need to while I'm doing an investigation. Mrs. Franklin, you are a material witness in a criminal case. Let's go."

"Don't move, Harriet," Noah snapped.

Trish wished there was some way she could stop him, but she was here as a deputy. Not a daughter.

Carter made eye contact with him. "Mr. Franklin, you have two choices. You may leave now. Or if you persist in obstructing my investigation, I'll charge you with that and take you into custody. Citizens are not allowed to block criminal investigations."

The two men stared at each other. "Deputy Franklin," Carter ordered her, "help your aunt into her coat and take her out to the car."

Trish stepped forward and took her aunt's arm to help her out of the kitchen chair. Her father lunged forward and pulled Trish's hand away from her aunt's arm.

Before Trish could react, the sheriff stepped between them. "You are Deputy Franklin's father, but that does not give you the right to strike an officer of the law. Now we are taking Mrs. Franklin in. Leave or I will arrest you."

Her father's long wrinkled face turned a mottled red-and-white. He tried to speak, his jaws working, but his words came out garbled.

"Dad, are you all right?" Trish asked, suddenly afraid he might be having a stroke.

Noah pushed past Harriet, bumping Trish hard. He stomped out the side door, slamming it behind him. Harriet swayed and Trish helped her sit down again.

The sheriff went to the side door and looked out, evidently making sure Noah had left. Trish heard her father's truck's distinctive rumble and rattle as it sped away. Carter came back in. "Mrs. Franklin, would you prefer that I take your statement here or at the—"

"Here," she gasped. "Please, here."

Trish quivered inside—worry over her father increased with each confrontation. She closed her eyes, drawing on her reserves.

"May I sit please?" Carter asked, as if the emotional scene he'd just witnessed hadn't taken place.

"Yes," Harriet said.

"Officer Franklin, why don't you warm up your aunt's coffee?"

Glad to do something, Trish moved to obey. She carried her aunt's cup to the counter where the old electric percolator sat. She freshened her aunt's coffee and then sat down in the chair her father had just vacated. Josh remained at the counter.

"Now," the sheriff began, "I take it that Noah told you that our department was on your property last night, investigating the recent rash of hit-and-runs?"

Harriet nodded, her lips pressed together to prevent tears, Trish thought.

Trish longed to pat her aunt's arm and reassure her that everything would be okay. But she was on duty and she didn't know herself if everything *would* be okay.

"Where were you last evening, Mrs. Franklin?" the sheriff asked.

"Here." Her aunt's word came out in a hoarse croak.

"And were you alone?"

"No, Hank Valliere was here," Harriet mumbled.

Hank here? Trish found that hard to believe.

"And Hank was here to do what?" Carter probed.

"He was asking permission to hunt on my land," Harriet said, staring into her coffee and her cheeks reddening.

Trish and the sheriff communicated silently with glances.

"Do you own the 1990 gray Oldsmobile sedan parked in the shed behind your hunting cabin?"

"That old thing?"

"Yes, is it yours? It doesn't have a current registration."

Harriet nodded, still focusing on her coffee. "Hasn't been driven in years."

"I'm sorry to say it has been driven by someone very recently," the sheriff replied. "Do you know who that could be?"

"I have no idea." Her head was down, but Harriet's voice was coming back to normal.

"Have you been out to the hunting shed in say the last month?"

"Why would I go out there?" Harriet's voice became firmer. "It's not huntin'season and I might not even hunt this year. Getting too old."

Trish again met Carter's eyes. Harriet's initial shock at their coming here was wearing off. And their chance of getting accurate and candid information was fading.

"Do you ever go out there, just to check things out?" Carter continued.

"No." Then Harriet met Carter's gaze defiantly. "It's too painful. With Jake gone. We'd still be hunting if it weren't for that Grey Lawson." Harriet's voice turned hard and mean. "Why aren't you out questioning him?"

"Grey Lawson was questioned last night."

"Then why are you bothering me?"

"Because it was your car that was driven last night and which forced Audra Blair off the road, injuring her."

This obviously surprised Aunt Harriet. Her blue eyes wide, she glanced at both of them in turn. "I didn't hear about Audra." Harriet betrayed herself with these words. "Is she okay?"

"Badly bruised and has a sprained wrist and whiplash, but she's home. I am going to have my deputy take your fingerprints now."

"Fingerprints?" Harriet yelped.

"We need to identify yours from all the ones we lifted last night from the vehicle, shed and cabin."

"You have no right—"

"We have every right," Carter cut her off. He waited while Josh followed his order, using an ink pad he'd pulled from his pocket. Though Trish took no part in any of this, Aunt Harriet scowled at her throughout the procedure. So much for being a comfort to her aunt.

"That's all for now, Mrs. Franklin. But I may return later with more questions." Carter rose, as did Trish. Josh already waited by the door.

"Why?" Harriet demanded, glaring at him. "This has nothing to do with me."

"Your vehicle appears to be the one used in the commission of four recent hit-and-runs. I'm afraid that involves you in this investigation."

"I'll get me a lawyer," Harriet threatened as Trish and Carter headed toward the side door.

"As you wish," Carter replied. "Tell him that I've instructed you not to leave the county without permission as you are a material witness in a criminal investigation."

"You can't tell me where I can and can't go," Harriet blustered.

Carter turned back just before shutting the door. "Mrs. Franklin, I can and I have. I'll be back." He closed the door behind them.

As they walked to his Jeep, Trish appreciated Carter's forbearance over the behavior of her contrary relatives.

One more time the memory of Grey's arms around her and his lips on hers shuddered through her, leaving her wanting his comfort more than ever. *God, I don't have a clue what's going on, but Grey has become special to me—right or wrong. Guard him from harm and suspicion. Lead us to the true culprit.*

GREY SAT IN THE NEARLY empty traditional-looking court-room with its abundance of polished oak and maple the next afternoon. Waiting for the judge to appear, Grey was not a happy camper. Court ranked second only as the very last place he ever wanted to be again, the first being prison. Somehow all the shame, dread and regret he'd experienced on the day he'd stood before a judge here rushed back like a swarm of mosquitoes, biting and stinging. How could it be as intense as if his own sentencing had been only days, not seven years, ago?

Yet here he was, sitting on a hard bench, trying not to fidget. Rae-Jean had called him and asked him to come to her sentencing and he hadn't been able to refuse her. Now he just wanted this to be over so he could leave for today's handyman job. He shifted in his seat, wishing he could be visible only to Rae-Jean.

There wouldn't be a full trial. Rae-Jean's lawyer had brokered a plea bargain. Rae-Jean would testify against her supplier at his trial and receive a lighter sentence on the drug charge. She still faced child abuse charges which the state would also pursue.

While Grey knew there was nothing he could do, he knew what it was like to face a judge. And from Trish, he knew that Rae-Jean's family would not come to show support for her. He didn't want Rae-Jean to be all alone with only a lawyer on her side of the court.

From his own experience of listening helplessly to his aunt's sobs while he was sentenced—he didn't really know which was worse. Having your family with you at your sentencing or being alone, either way was torture.

The lush memory of Trish in his arms zipped through his mind, leaving him achingly alone. Why had she come to Elsie's? Why had he kissed her as she'd asked? Had he been temporarily insane?

From where Rae-Jean sat at the front of the courtroom, she turned around to face Grey and mouthed, "Thanks for coming."

He nodded. Then he heard heavy footsteps and Harold from NA took a place beside Grey. They exchanged subdued greetings.

"All rise." The bailiff announced the judge's arrival.

Grey heard another set of lighter footsteps and glanced over his shoulder. Trish in her uniform had walked in and taken a place across the aisle from him and Harold. Embarrassment sizzled through Grey.

Until Trish's entrance, he'd been merely uncomfortable. Now he was nonplussed. With her in her deputy uniform and he in his work clothes, it underscored the enormous gap between them. She was a law officer, an official agent for the county. He was an ex-con, a handyman. *And I kissed her two nights ago.*

All the sensations of holding her surged through him. He wrenched his mind away from that rich tactile memory. The possible consequences of their recent kisses churned inside him with barbs that ripped at his pride.

⸻

THE COURT PROCEEDINGS began and were over within minutes. Rae-Jean Franklin, first-time drug offender, would go to a state drug offender facility farther south to get clean. She'd serve a short sentence in a women's facility and then be on probation for a year. As an officer led her away back to the county jail, Rae-Jean looked dazed.

Trish crossed the aisle to Harold and Grey. "I thought someone from my family should attend," she murmured. "Plus I had to be here on other business." She nodded once and walked out.

Grey watched her leave, an intense sense of loss filtering through each nerve. In Elsie's kitchen, she had sought comfort in his arms. Here in public, she'd treated him as a mere acquaintance. That was the way it had to be. The way it would be.

HE SAT ON THE SIDE of his bed and shuddered whenever he thought of the sound of that siren behind him on Cross-cut Road. He'd raced back to the shed to ditch the sedan. To get rid of his connection to it. And then he'd lost his nerve.

He'd called 911 from the public phone outside the welcome center to report the accident. In his panic, all he'd thought of was pushing the blame away from himself. But now he couldn't use the sedan again.

Fool. Idiot. Now you've done it.

Had the fact that he'd quickly wiped off the steering wheel and door handles with his shirttail been enough? Had he left any other prints in the sedan? But he'd never been arrested before so they wouldn't have his prints on file, right? But still... *Why didn't I wear gloves?*

He hunched over with his arms around himself. Stark fear sawed at him with a ragged blade. *Now what do I do? I have to get rid of Grey Lawson. I ruined everything last night. Why didn't I keep my head?*

A tidal wave of dread rose within him. Grey Lawson had to be driven out of Winfield. *I'll never have a minute's peace with him here. But how do I do it?*

Chapter 10

Two days had passed since Trish had witnessed Carter interviewing her aunt in her home. Now Trish sat in a sheriff's department bare interrogation room under a fluorescent light and faced Lamar Valliere. Lamar had graduated high school with her younger brother, Mick, and he'd been laid off at the paper mill with Chaney. In blue jeans and a red knit shirt and his black hair pulled back into a short ponytail today, Lamar slouched in his chair, glaring at her. This was the second time she had interviewed him about the hit-and-run incidents. Would she get anything useful from him today?

"So, Lamar, you're sticking with your story that you were at Harriet's house *with your father* on the night of the latest hit-and-run?" she asked for the fifth time, trying to mask her frustration.

"Yeah." Lamar's tone had begun and remained belligerent.

As best she could, Trish ignored his tone and asked in her professional voice, "We have interviewed patrons of Bugsy's Tavern on the night in question." Interrogation often wore a suspect down until he let something slip in the anger of a moment. Would Lamar?

"So?"

Or would Lamar's stubbornness wear her down? "We have sworn statements from several customers that you were at Bugsy's that night from around six p.m. until closing."

"They're mistaken." He sneered at her.

He was mocking her and she pushed down hard on her escalating irritation with him, with this case. "I'm afraid we can prove that you were there by these eyewitness accounts." *We know you're lying.*

"A bunch of drunks as eyewitnesses?" he snorted. "It's their word against mine and you know it."

Might as well lay it on the line then. "Why are you lying? If you were there and others will testify to it, you have an alibi for the latest hit-and-run." Would even self-interest move Lamar? "I don't get it or you."

"I was at Harriet's that evening with my dad. That's all I'm saying. Either charge me with something or I'm leaving."

He was bluffing and she knew it. She had taken Lamar over and over the same ground for an hour. Lamar had repeated over and over the same rehearsed lies. And the result? *She* was the one coming undone. And she didn't want to admit it but her feelings for Grey were the source of her exasperation. Lamar wasn't just lying; he was lying in order to hurt Grey. To cast suspicion on him.

She rose, her face a cool mask, her emotions a swirling mass. "I'll be right back." She escaped, locking the door behind her. If she didn't put some space between them, she might go for Lamar's deceitful throat.

Down the hall at the sheriff's office door, she glanced in through its window. Seated behind his desk, Carter was questioning Hank Valliere, lounging across from him, for the second time, as well. Carter nodded for her to enter. She'd hoped that Carter had made some progress. But as soon as she entered the room, an atmosphere of tension and antagonism slapped her like an insult.

"Hank," Carter said as Trish shut the door behind herself, "we know you weren't at Harriet's the night of the latest hit-and-run."

"How's that?"

She hung back near the door.

"You were home alone that evening," Carter continued doggedly. "We questioned your neighbors and they will testify that your truck was outside your house all evening until dark."

Trish noted the sheriff's jaw was clenched. Did that mean Hank was just as obstinate as Lamar?

"They're right." Hank cast her a nasty gloating glance. "I was at Harriet's with my son, Lamar. He picked me up with his truck."

"Your neighbors said that no one came to your house that night."

"They're mistaken."

Trish recognized the same practiced phrase that Lamar had used repeatedly. It was a clever phrase because it didn't call the witnesses liars, just people who'd made a mistake. She folded her arms and leaned back against the wall. Perhaps looking unconcerned would smooth the sharp edge off her temper.

"We have phone records showing that Noah Franklin called you on the night in question." Carter held up a sheet of paper.

"So what does that prove?" Hank shifted in his chair, shooting her another smug look.

The sheriff continued, "Your home phone records show that this was the first time that you have received a call from Noah in the past six months."

"I have an answering machine." Hank shrugged. "If Noah called, it would have picked up for me. I wasn't home."

"But why would Noah call you that night?"

"Why shouldn't he?"

Listening to someone she'd known all her life, known as an honest person, tell out-and-out lies to another law enforcement officer was rubbing her nerves raw. In Madison, she'd never known any of her victims or lawbreakers personally. Here she did. *And I don't like it one bit.*

Carter pressed his lips together. "Also after the hit-and-run, you called Harriet Franklin that evening for the first time in six months."

"I didn't need to talk to her until it was near huntin' season," Hank said, staring at Carter as if taunting him.

"Why would you call her *and* go over to her house at such a late hour?" Carter pressed.

Trish felt like telling him to save his breath. Evidently, Hank, Lamar, Noah and Harriet had decided to join together to protect the one of them who was responsible for the hit-and-runs. Their stories all echoed each other, sometimes word for word.

"I wanted to make sure," Hank lied patently glib, "that she was home before Lamar and I went over."

"Harriet's neighbors will testify that your truck never parked anywhere near her house on the night in question."

Hank held out both his upturned palms. "It's a black truck. Hard to see at night."

"I thought you said that Lamar picked you up and drove you to Harriet's?"

Hank surged forward in his seat, for the first time betraying his irritation. "You can't trick me that easy. Lamar's truck is black, too. I was thinking of his truck." Hank looked over at Trish. "Her brother Chaney's truck is black, too. Why don't you ask him where he was on *the night in question?*" Hank said the final four words with snide sarcasm.

"Then you do not want to alter your previous statement?" the sheriff asked with a controlled politeness Trish envied.

"No, I don't." Hank stood. "So charge me with something or I'm leaving."

Trish had expected this and again Hank mimicked Lamar's words. She flashed Carter a look, telling him that Lamar had given her the same ultimatum.

"Very well, Hank. For now," Carter said. "Don't leave the county as I'll probably be questioning you again."

Hank pushed past her. Trish, followed by Carter, walked the few steps to the interrogation room where she unlocked the door for Lamar. The sheriff gave him the same warning as Hank. The two left, aiming disdainful looks at Trish and Carter over their shoulders.

Trish followed Carter back to his office and took the chair Hank had just vacated. She needed to go somewhere and let off steam, maybe scream for a few minutes. She rubbed her moist palms on the top of her thighs.

"What did you get out of Lamar?" Carter asked.

"Nothing new." Trish held back angry words that still clogged her throat.

Carter grimaced. "They're sticking like glue to those alibis."

"Those well-rehearsed alibis," Trish agreed. And silently added, *Probably written and coordinated by my father.* The worst hadn't happened yet. She hadn't had to or been forced to watch Carter bring her own father in for questioning. She knew that her father would go to jail before he would give in. Would this string of dangerous games end before that final calamity occurred?

"I've questioned your aunt's whereabouts for the first three hit-and-runs."

Trish had expected this, but she still dreaded the answer she'd receive. "Yes?"

"By some strange fluke she was with your father on all three of those evenings." Carter looked apologetic since he'd just stated in effect that her father and aunt were lying in concert.

She didn't make any reply to this. But she admitted, "My father is worrying me. This vendetta against Grey is taking its toll on him. He doesn't attend church as he has done all his life. He looks like he's losing weight. I heard *unofficially* from someone who works at his doctor's office that he has blown off his latest appointment for his heart."

Sudden fatigue swept through her like a storm front, knocking out her power. *Lord, where is this all going to end?*

"I'm sorry," Carter said, looking down at his blotter. "Do you think your father has a role in this?"

"You mean the hit-and-runs themselves or just in obstructing our investigation?" She bowed her heavy head.

"Both." He nudged a pen in line with the others on his blotter.

"About the latter—yes. About the incidents themselves—I just don't know." Acid churned in her stomach. She'd never before conceived the idea of having to arrest a member of her own family. And her father? *No. Please. No.*

Carter looked up. "Well, we have circumstantial evidence that Hank and Lamar were not at Harriet's that evening. But it's fuzzy and still doesn't give us the identity of the guilty party we're after."

Trish nodded, her head in one hand. Who's doing this? Is my father or aunt the culprit? Or are they shielding someone else? And how can we stop whoever it is before someone gets seriously hurt...or killed?

———

AFTER WORK THAT EVENING, Trish drove down Cross-cut to her trailer, caught between conflicting urges. One part of her wanted to go home, pack her things and move back to

Madison. The other part was pushing for her to confront her father and try one more time to reason with him.

At the last moment the latter won out. She turned into the lane to her dad's house, not the one to her trailer. If nothing else, she had to confront her dad about not keeping his doctor's appointment. When she reached the house, she knew she'd made the wrong turn.

Noah was standing on his front steps, berating Pastor Ray. "I don't need you telling me what to do!"

Trish would have turned around, but both men looked over and saw her then. Her father charged down the steps toward her SUV.

"You!" he shouted. "Go home! I don't want to see your disloyal face! That my own daughter would side against family. Everyone's talking about you and that Lawson! You're disgusting."

I'm not turning tail and running. Trish got out and stood, using the open driver's door as a shield. "What's happening, Pastor Ray?"

Pastor Ray walked over to her. "Hello, Trish. I'm sorry I haven't had better luck. I came here to ask your father to put aside his enmity toward Grey and come—"

"I won't step inside that church until that Lawson leaves," Noah stated.

Trish flushed with embarrassment. She didn't know what to say to the pastor or her father. It was a no-win situation. She decided to just go ahead and question her father about the missed appointment. It couldn't do any more harm. "Dad, I wanted to know how your last appointment with Dr. Bell went?" *I moved home to see that you took better care of yourself.*

"None of your business! You're not my nurse!"

She had expected this reply, but it didn't make it any more welcome. Her father gave new meaning to the phrase, "Waging a losing battle."

Pastor Ray turned to face Noah. "Hatred and bitterness only hurts the person who harbors them. You're hurting yourself physically and spiritually—"

"That's my business. Grey Lawson killed my twin brother. The person in the whole world I was closest to. And I'm not forgetting or forgiving. An eye for an eye."

Noah's words sickened Trish. First her father had lost Trish's mom and then Jake. Both losses had crippled him deep inside in some horrible way. *Where is the man who once loved me, tickled me and made me squeal with laughter?*

"You know that you are misquoting the Bible," Pastor Ray said mildly. "And I think it would be advisable for you to seek some sort of counseling before you break down—"

Red in the face, Noah charged away from them and into his house. The door slammed.

Trish looked to the pastor. "Sorry," she muttered.

"You have nothing to apologize for." Pastor Ray put on his hat. "I wasn't at this pastorate when your mother died. But from what I hear, your father underwent a complete change then."

Trish nodded.

"Well, I tried today. I have to be getting home for supper." He nodded at Trish. "I'll keep your father in my prayers."

"Thanks," Trish whispered. She got into her SUV and drove away, too. What could any of them do for her dad but pray? His frame of mind, and maybe his health, were deteriorating before her eyes. With no end, no happy end in sight.

Then one of her father's taunts came back to her. "Everyone's talking about you and that Lawson!" Was that just a means to hurt her or was it true? And if it was, what should she, could she do about it?

ANDY AND PENNY FRANKLIN had called and invited Elsie for Sunday dinner. So here Grey was helping his aunt out of the Chrysler in front of Andy's sprawling ranch home on Cross-cut Road. Grey then recognized two other vehicles parked at Andy's, Chaney's black pickup. Grey hadn't wanted to come in the first place and now he saw that it was going to be a family affair. He nearly backed out and told Elsie that he'd pick her up later.

The day's harsh autumn wind, a prequel of what would be coming in another month, snatched Elsie's pink chiffon scarf from her head and Grey had to run and catch it.

The front door opened and Andy said, "What about that wind?" and Grey missed his chance to escape. Inside, Andy hung their coats in the foyer closet. Grey hung back, wishing he could come up with a way to leave that wouldn't upset or reflect poorly on Elsie.

"We're so glad you could come." Penny looked out from the kitchen doorway. Her two little girls flanked her, one on each side looking curiously at Grey and Elsie. Wonderful fragrances drifted down the hall to Grey. He analyzed them and identified them as baking yeast rolls, roasting chicken, melting butter, and something with cinnamon and apples. Prison food had never smelled like this.

"Thanks for asking us," Elsie said, beaming.

Grey, still trying to remain unnoticed in the background, merely nodded. The delicious cooking aromas had made him instantly hungry. His stomach betrayed him by rumbling loudly.

Young Jake charged out of the living room where Grey heard Packers football being discussed on TV. The boy threw his arms around Grey's waist. "Hi! My daddy and I are here to eat dinner, too. Aunt Penny's mashed potatoes are the best."

Grey ruffled Jake's blond bangs. "Hey, pal."

With a can of soda pop in hand, Chaney leaned against the

arched doorway to the living room. "Come on. It's pregame stuff."

Young Jake led Grey into the living room, which was beige and white with touches of forest green. One wall was dominated by a fireplace and in another corner, a thin tabletop TV perched on an antique sewing machine. Trish already sat on a love seat. She gave him a tense apologetic smile. The ridiculous idea that Trish's family was matchmaking raced through his mind. He rejected it, but the feeling persisted. *Surely not.*

Penny led Elsie out into the kitchen. Andy sat back down in his armchair and Young Jake and Chaney took over the sofa. Grey swallowed a grimace and took the only open spot, the one beside Trish. Trish's brothers could not be pushing Trish and him together, so that could only mean they must be clueless about Grey's attraction to Trish. *And I better keep it that way.*

He tried to keep his focus on the talking heads on TV, but his eyes insisted on tracking Trish's movements. She wasn't doing anything that should have caught his interest, she was just sitting there. He smelled that distinctive fragrance she wore, something spicy that suited her. And her auburn hair appeared to capture and radiate with all the light in the room.

Penny brought out a can of soda pop for Grey and promised that dinner would be ready and eaten before the game actually started. A can in hand, Grey worked at consciously maintaining the few inches that separated him from Trish.

The pregame show ended and Young Jake ran out to see what was happening in the kitchen. "I took Jake to see his mom yesterday," Chaney said softly.

Grey did not want to discuss the boy and Rae-Jean here. He wished he could just announce, "I don't know anything about kids," and then everyone would leave him alone. But of course he couldn't. He knew that Andy and Chaney were showing him friendship. In light of past and present events, he couldn't ignore that.

In fact, something inside him had warmed when he'd come inside and heard their unmistakably sincere welcomes. It was almost like being part of a real family, something he'd never experienced. Someday in the future, he might finally have a family of his own, but not now. *And I'm never going to be a member of this family.*

Trish shifted on her cushion. Suddenly her hip pocket was against his. Surely, she hadn't done that on purpose? He tried to ease away from her without making a big deal out of it.

"How did the visit go?" Grey asked Chaney, trying to keep the focus off him and Trish.

Chaney shrugged. "Okay, I guess. I did what you said, you know, about not letting Rae make excuses."

Grey nodded. Either gravity or Trish was making it impossible for him to regain those few inches of safety. His discomfort mounted.

"Rae didn't like it at first," Chaney continued. "I could see she wanted to tell me to shut up. But she got real quiet and then told Jake that I was right."

"That sounds positive," Andy put in. "Taking responsibility for one's actions is the first step in moving forward from any mess."

Grey nodded, hoping the discussion would end here. And that he could ease away from Trish. But then Penny called them all to the kitchen. Grey was the first one on his feet.

"You must be hungry," Andy chortled.

Grey felt his neck warm, but merely followed Trish to the table.

"We don't have a separate dining room," Penny said as she directed Grey to the seat beside Trish at the long table in the large country kitchen. "I think a nice large kitchen should be the center of the home."

Grey sat down after making certain that Trish and the other ladies were seated. Why did they appear to persist in pushing Trish and him together?

"We like to join hands for grace," Andy said and took his wife's and Elsie's hands.

Trish took Grey's hand in her soft one and Andy began the prayer. Touching Trish again distracted him from paying attention to grace. His mind was behaving like a camera, moving in and out of focus on the gathering.

Amens were said around the table and she let go of his hand. He took a deep breath. The meal wouldn't last long and then he would take Elsie home. *I just have to keep my cool a little longer.*

After eating more chicken, mashed potatoes, green beans, cloverleaf rolls and apple pie than he thought could possibly fit into his stomach, the desire to take a nap settled over him. After the meal though, everyone pitched in, scraping dishes and filling the dishwasher and wiping the table and counters. There was laughter and banter.

Grey let it all soak in, let it settle deep inside him so that in some private moment, he could take it out and relive it, savor the experience.

Glancing at the wall clock, Andy announced, "Time for the game."

Grey opened his mouth to announce he'd be taking Elsie home when his aunt piped up with, "Oh, this is just what I needed. I haven't watched a Packers game with friends for a long time. It's so much more fun then."

Grey silently gave in and joined everyone in the living room. Chaney and Jake moved to the floor, ceding the sofa to Elsie and Penny and the two little girls. Grey again took his place next to Trish on the love seat.

All around him, the Packers fans cheered their team as they took the yardage on Lambeau Field in Green Bay. Grey found that Trish still fascinated him more than the fiercely competitive game. He found himself breathing in time with her and listening to the cadence of her voice as she shouted and groaned over the game.

For a few moments, he let himself toy with the illusion that he was a part of this family. Then he pondered why Noah wanted to keep himself apart from this happy Sunday afternoon.

Noah Franklin had a great family and yet had rejected them, while Grey would have given anything to be a part of such a group. Grey knew that Noah would blame the breach in his family on Grey. But Noah had to take some responsibility. His estrangement from his family wasn't all due to Jake's death seven years ago. Trish had revealed that it had started long before that. *It isn't all my fault.* A startling idea.

Evening had fallen by the time the Packers won. Then, finally, Grey was able to rise and announce that he'd be taking Elsie home.

"Would you drop Trish home?" Chaney asked. "Andy needs help with some wallpapering upstairs. Now that I'm working at the high school nights, my time is limited."

Trish blushed and wouldn't look at Grey.

This let him know that, yes, she, too, was aware of her family's less-than-subtle matchmaking. But there was no way to avoid driving her home.

As Grey drove away, Young Jake and Penny stood at the door waving goodbye. "I'm so glad that Chaney got a job," Elsie said. "So many others are still looking."

Grey let Trish, sitting in the backseat behind Elsie, respond. He had enough to do, driving while fighting off the aftereffects of sitting at her side all afternoon.

When Elsie's log cabin came into view, his aunt said with an undeceiving innocence in her voice, "Grey, why don't you drop me off and then take Trish on home? Bucky's barking for his supper."

Grey was not fooled for one second. Bucky could wait. Elsie, along with Trish's brothers, was matchmaking. But again, what could he do? Without comment, he pulled up the bumpy drive while he did a slow burn. He'd have to take a stand and soon. He helped Aunt Elsie out and into the house. While Trish took her place in the front seat. "I'll be right back, Auntie," he said.

"Don't hurry!" Elsie waved and went inside, switching on the kitchen lights.

The treetops still bent with the wind. Grey drove back onto the main road in silence. Now if Trish would just let him take her home without any discussion. But that was probably too much to ask. In this very car, Trish had twisted his sleeve, demanding he face the fact that she was attracted to him. *Not today, Trish. Don't rock the boat.* But he braced himself.

When Trish did speak, her topic took him by surprise. "I want to thank you for whatever you said to Chaney about Rae-Jean and Young Jake. My brother's been a lot calmer and Young Jake is adjusting better to his new routine of staying with Florence on school nights. I even think Chaney will take Jake down to see his mom when she's moved to one of the drug rehabilitation centers in Chippewa Falls."

Grey nodded, gauging the last few miles between their houses, passing swiftly. *Not too much farther.*

"Thanks, Grey."

"No problem." *Almost there.*

"So did you expect that level of matchmaking today?"

He clenched his jaw. He'd nearly made it to her house. "Do you always have to put everything into words?" he growled. "Can't you just ignore some things?"

"No, I'm not good at ignoring things," she replied lightly, as if they were discussing favorite ice cream flavors.

An understatement of mammoth proportions.

"And that's a plus in my line of work," Trish pointed out.

"This isn't about work." *Now drop it, Trish, please.*

"You didn't answer my question. How do we handle the fact that our families are trying to throw us together?"

"I for one am going to ignore it."

For once, she didn't appear to have a response. She merely nodded. Was that good or bad?

Her lane came in sight. *Home free!* He drove up to her steps and waited for her to get out. *No more talk, Trish. Just say thanks and good-night.* She didn't move. He made to open his door to come around.

But she stopped him with her hand on his elbow. "I can get out myself."

But she didn't get out. He waited, staring straight ahead. *Please, go in, Trish. Don't stir the waters again.*

She scooted over to his side and perched on her knees on the bench seat. "Good night, Grey." And she kissed him. On the lips.

He couldn't resist. He kissed her in return. Oh, Trish's enticing lips. He was rendered mute, mellowed to putty.

She finally lifted her lips a fraction from his. "When all this is over," she murmured and then she was out and running up her metal steps, making them rattle.

He turned his car around and headed home, still feeling her lips on his and wondering what her final words meant. *When this is over...what?*

⊂⊐

TWO MORNINGS LATER ON TUESDAY, Grey waited in the basement of the town hall where he was working as a volunteer at the food pantry. Those who needed food assistance were lined up in an S-pattern around the room and up the steps.

Grey was surprised at some of the people in line, particularly Eddie. He hadn't realized how hard a time his friend was having to make ends meet. But Eddie was only working at the convenience store. He still lived in the same one-room basement apartment he had before the accident. And since Eddie still spent most of his evenings at Bugsy's Tavern, it wasn't hard to figure out where most of his income went.

Many of the people in line were those who'd been laid off from the paper mill. And one of them in particular worried him. Lamar Valliere. Grey hoped that there wouldn't be a public scene. He was so tired of being dumped on in public. He deserved it, but today, his self-control felt as flimsy as a finely spun spider web.

Along with Sylvie Patterson, another volunteer, Grey now was waiting to distribute the perishables, such as cheeses, fresh fruit, vegetables and cured meats, which had been delivered this morning by the government and local producers. After the recipients picked up their paper bag of boxed and canned goods, they would come to him and Sylvie for the final items. She'd smiled in welcome at Grey and explained the routine. Most of the people in line kept their eyes down, which Grey understood. Charity was hard to take for most people. Perhaps Lamar wouldn't even look up.

People began moving through the line, picking up their bags and stopping at the perishables table. Grey tried not to show any emotion. But the people who came to his table gave him a variety of looks, disapproving, curious, cautious. Then Lamar, obviously spoiling for a fight, was in front of him. All hope of Lamar ignoring him vanished. Grey braced himself.

"So you're doing your good deed, are you?"

Grey saw Tom was trying to break away from an older man who was explaining something with his hands. Grey ignored the taunt and handed Lamar a plastic shopping bag with an assortment of foods.

"Look at me. Don't you dare ignore me," Lamar ordered Grey.

Tom was still trying to get away from the older man. Grey looked straight into Lamar's eyes. He could fight his own battles without Tom's aid. Grey had finally had enough of public humiliation. "Lamar, I truly regret what happened seven years ago, but that doesn't change anything. And bad-mouthing me won't bring Darleen back."

Lamar opened his mouth, but Eddie came up beside him. "Hey, cut Grey some slack."

Lamar turned on Eddie then. "You're as bad as him. You were there. You could have stopped him—" Lamar swung his head toward Grey "—from driving drunk. But you didn't. You're just as responsible for Darleen's death—"

"If we follow that line of thinking," Tom said, coming up behind Eddie, "then Darleen is just as responsible for her death. She could have refused to get in the car that night. It's time you considered that."

Lamar took a swing at Tom. Tom ducked and Lamar clipped Eddie's jaw. Grey's friend dropped to the floor, out cold.

"I think you'd better leave," Tom stated, "or I'll call the police."

Lamar picked up his bag of groceries and threw it at Grey. Then he stomped away, up the stairs past the line.

Grey and Tom helped Eddie up off the floor and onto a chair. Eddie took a few minutes to surface completely. He blinked. "Never could take a hit to the jaw. I told you that first day, man, you shouldn't have come back here."

Grey couldn't speak. Eddie had taken the blow which Grey felt had really been meant for him. Which was worse—taking the abuse himself or watching a friend take it for him? Right now he knew the answer. It had been harder to see Eddie hit the linoleum. *I shouldn't have said anything to Lamar. I should have just taken it.*

But if this didn't stop soon, he might have to ask Elsie to move away with him. Between those who wanted his head and those who were busy matchmaking Grey and Trish, Grey's peace of mind hung in limp rags and tatters.

━━

THE SCENE AT THE FOOD PANTRY had hit the gossip grapevine with a vengeance and it strengthened his nerve. He'd get his revenge. He'd make it impossible for Grey to stay. One more game of chicken. And he knew just whom he wanted to target. This time it would work. This time it would split everything wide-open and force Grey Lawson out of Winfield.

Chapter 11

That night, Grey had just drifted off to sleep when he heard the pounding on the back door. He glanced at the luminous digital clock by his bed. Who would be visiting at nearly midnight?

Suddenly Grey jerked up wide-awake, his galloping heart thumping against his breastbone. Had there been another game of chicken? Had the sheriff and Trish come to question him again? *No, not again.* Cool liquid dread leaked into every cell of his body. He got up and stumbled to the door, hoping he could answer it before the knocking woke Elsie. But Bucky was there before him, barking at the door. Grey opened it, braced to face the sheriff and Trish for one more awful round of demeaning questions.

To his surprise, though, it was Chaney Franklin who stood at the door. "I'm sorry. I know it's too late. I'm really sorry, but I need to talk to someone—" Chaney's voice broke "—and you're the only one who might understand, help."

Grey tried to wrap his mind around Chaney's totally unexpected arrival and his ominous words. Grey scrubbed his face with one hand. Sudden fear hit him like a karate chop. "Is it Young Jake? Is he all right?"

"Jake's fine. He's safe at Florence's sleeping. Please, can I come in?"

Grey moved back into the dimly lit kitchen where he kept having these late-night sessions. Chaney came in, still wearing his khaki work clothes. "Coffee?" Grey mumbled. "Want me to put some on?"

Chaney collapsed onto a chair at the table; his clasped hands worked as if he were twisting something within them. Then Chaney laid his face down on the table and wept.

Shocked and horrified, Grey just stood in the middle of the room, immobilized.

"Grey," Elsie said, entering the kitchen wearing her worn robe, "go ahead and make that coffee."

Bucky left Grey and padded to Elsie's side. "Auntie," Grey started, "let me handle this. You need your sleep—"

"Grey, make the coffee, please." Elsie sat down at a right angle to Chaney. Bucky lay down under the table with a sigh. Elsie began stroking Chaney's shoulder and murmuring words of encouragement.

Watching this prompted a potent memory. Grey's mind dragged him back to the first time she'd visited him in jail. As he'd sobbed out his regret and shame, she'd performed the same kindness for him, patting his shoulder, comforting him with her unchanging affection. Strong reactions to this memory filled him, threatening to unman him. Grey turned his back, giving Chaney some measure of privacy. He went through the process of getting a pot of coffee on the stove. What could have happened to Chaney since Sunday?

By the time the pot started percolating, Chaney was finally sitting up straight again, wiping his eyes with his hands. "Sorry about that."

Elsie patted his shoulder again. "Now tell us. What's upset you so?"

Yes, what is this all about? Yet Grey already dreaded what Chaney had come to reveal. He remained in the shadows, protecting himself from what was coming.

Chaney leaned his elbows on the table and cupped his face in both hands as if he couldn't face them while speaking aloud the words he'd come to say. "I got a call from Rae-Jean just before I dropped Jake off at Florence's tonight." He paused as if reinforcing his control. "She told me that she'd just been seen by the doctor at the drug rehabilitation facility that she's been sent to south of here."

Braced, Grey leaned back against the kitchen counter and waited, knowing that Rae-Jean hadn't called with good news. But how bad would it be?

"The doctor examined her and confirmed to her that she is a little over four months pregnant." With his face still buried, Chaney began to shake again, but made no sound.

"Is the baby yours?" Elsie asked in a matter-of-fact voice.

"It might be." Chaney wiped his damp face with a paper napkin Elsie handed him. "Around four months ago, she came home for a few weeks, telling me she wanted to try for reconciliation. I took her back and then I came home one night from work, told her I was going to be laid off. She left me the next day for good." A trace of bitterness slipped into the final sentence.

For several minutes, the only sounds in the kitchen were the snuffling of Bucky at Elsie's feet and the bubbling of the percolator. Grey couldn't think of a single word of comfort or counsel. *What can we possibly do for you, Chaney?*

Then Elsie asked, "Was she taking drugs at that time?"

"Yes."

Grey let the dreadful one-word answer sink deep into him.

He knuckled his tired eyes again, aware of a deep tide of sympathy. What did meth do to a forming embryo?

"The doctor suggested...an abortion," Chaney replied. "She's pretty broken up. She begged my forgiveness and said she just wished she could go back and relive this year. So she could erase all the stupid decisions she'd made."

Grey knew how that felt all too deeply. Wishing he could blot out that one fateful night in his life had dogged him for the first year he was in prison. And at times, it still popped up. Especially when Trish was near him. He shoved this train of thought aside. *Rae-Jean, life is the way we make it until we let God in to change it. Some people may forgive. But no one ever lets you forget.*

"It's a good sign that she said *she* had made those decisions," Elsie pointed out. "Every child can be a blessing and this child could be a special blessing to her."

"In prison?" Chaney asked with obvious disbelief.

"Yes, a baby could provide her with added incentive to get her life back on the straight and narrow." Elsie glanced at the stove. "Why don't you pour us that coffee, Grey? We don't want it too strong at this hour."

Grey obeyed and finally eased down across from Chaney at the small kitchen table, grateful that Elsie seemed to know how to comfort Chaney.

"If this baby is yours," Elsie asked, "could you accept it, Chaney?"

"I could. But what kind of problems will it have? And Rae-Jean and I might never get back together. After all that she's put me and Jake through—and for no good reason—I don't know if we can ever put it back together again."

"Has Rae-Jean ever given you a reason for her getting into drugs?"

Chaney took a sip of steaming coffee. "She told me life just got to be work, work, work—at her job, at home, and helping me finish the inside of our house. She said all of a sudden one day all she wanted was fun."

"And she thought meth would be fun?" Grey asked, his tone dripping with stark disbelief.

Chaney held up one palm. "Personally I think that she sort of lost her mind. The guy who became her supplier...and more —" he gritted his teeth, looking as if he was getting ready to snarl "—had started hanging around the café she worked at in Ashford. Flirting with her, you know?"

"Yes, I know," Elsie said with a sad nod. "Wives can at times be very susceptible to flattery from a charming new man. Some men can sense when a woman is susceptible to straying and take advantage of it. Rae-Jean is so pretty. And I'm sure he wanted to hook her to him with drugs, control her. Some men like to do that, debase an honest woman. It gives them a feeling of power and satisfaction at pulling someone good down to their level. And I'm sure he felt that he'd rubbed your face into the dirt, too."

Grey looked at his aunt in the dim light. Every word she spoke rang with truth. And such understanding. Suddenly he wanted to open a subject that had remained taboo—at his insistence—for many years. Grey wanted to know what had happened to send his mother from him. At twelve, he'd been so angry, so crushed that he'd refused to let Elsie speak his mother's name. And his mother had never told him exactly why his father had left town the year before she did. What had happened to his own family?

"What should I do?" Chaney muttered.

Good question, Grey commented silently.

Elsie sighed. "I don't think there is much you can do. Rae-Jean will be the one who decides whether to end this pregnancy or not. Even as the probable father, you won't be asked for an opinion. But if Rae-Jean does choose to have this baby, there is one thing that I don't think has occurred to you that you must keep in mind."

"What's that?" Chaney's voice clearly announced that he feared the answer he'd receive.

"If this child is born, it will be Jake's brother or sister, full or half. And don't ever make the mistake that that doesn't mean much. The connection between siblings can be quite strong even when they have been parted. The bond of blood is one of the strongest bonds between humans. Don't leave Jake out of this. He won't thank you if you do."

"You mean I should ask him what he thinks about this?" Chaney's shock was evident. Grey felt the same aversion.

"No, but don't leave him out of the loop," Elsie continued. "If Rae-Jean decides to terminate, then he shouldn't be told about this until he is an adult, if ever. But if she keeps the child, he will want to know that child. And you will have to permit that."

"And it might be his full brother or sister," Chaney commented as if to himself alone.

"Yes, the child might be. And if it is, it's yours just as much as Jake's." Elsie took a deep breath. "Chaney, you are in the position to do great good or great harm to Jake, Rae-Jean, this baby and yourself. Don't react with anger. Now *you* are the one with choices to make, far-reaching, life-changing ones. Don't ever let that thought get away from you. And you'll need prayer and lots of it."

―――

THE NEXT EVENING TRISH waited while the phone rang— once, twice. She twisted the phone cord as she sat at the built-in table in her trailer. The window beside her let in a pleasant evening breeze. Warm weather and golden sunset should have cheered her.

Grey's voice came over the line. "Hello, Ryerson's."

"Hi, Grey, this is Trish."

Silence.

A daunting response. She sighed inwardly. *Just call me intrepid.* "I called to thank you for helping Chaney again."

"Oh."

"He met me for lunch at Trina's today and told me all about Rae-Jean."

"Good."

Trish pursed her lips. Wasn't Grey carrying the strong and silent type a little too far? "I'm glad he's found someone to help him through this."

"Elsie was the one who had the answers," Grey replied, sounding defensive. "I didn't."

"Your aunt is a wise woman."

"No argument here."

Trish braced herself for conflict. "I'd like to have you and Elsie over for supper sometime soon."

A silent pause. Then, "Trish, you know that isn't a good idea." Another significant pause. "We need to—"

"To what?" Suddenly she was angry, white-hot. "To cave in to my father's bad temper and irrational behavior?"

"We've gone over this before. There are too many solid reasons we should stay away from each other. Goodbye, Trish." And he had the nerve to cut the connection.

Trish banged the receiver against the tabletop as if punishing Grey. Had a more stubborn man than Grey Lawson ever been born? She dialed Elsie's number a second time. When Grey answered again, she barked, "I'm not giving up on you, Grey Lawson. Get that through your thick skull. And you and Elsie are invited to my trailer for Saturday night supper and that's that." Then she hung up—fuming. *I will not give in to my father's obsession. Or into Grey's mindset of guilt.*

▭

THE NEXT MORNING, TRISH couldn't believe her eyes. Along with the two other deputies that had helped Carter with the crime scene investigation of the gray sedan and surroundings, she stared at the clear evidence bag sitting on the sheriff's desk. The bag was marked and sealed. Inside it was a button obviously torn from a shirt since a small swatch of flannel fabric still clung to the button.

"I cannot believe that this bag got dropped at the crime scene. And that no one missed it when we cataloged all the evidence," Carter said in a menacing voice which predicted that someone's head might roll. And soon.

"I lifted this from the doorjamb of the gray sedan. It was caught on the latch there," the youngest deputy, Josh Hayden, admitted, flushing up red.

Stern faced, Carter stared at the deputy. "Why didn't you tell us that it was missing when we got back to the station and went over the list of evidence we collected?"

"I...I..." the young officer stuttered.

Unable to bear the younger man's disgrace in silence, Trish spoke up. "That was the day your wife was put on bed rest, wasn't she?"

"Yeah, but her pregnancy shouldn't have affected my performance," Josh said, hanging his head. "I'm sorry, sir."

Carter visibly let the irritation drain from his expression and the tense way he'd held his shoulders. "None of us are perfect. Just don't let it happen again. Fortunately, I found this when the wrecker and I went to impound the sedan. And fortunately, the wrecker saw me open the door and pick it up from under the sedan's front seat and it was still sealed. So it should stand up in court as incontestable evidence. Now, if we can find a match to this fabric on a shirt missing a button, we could have our culprit."

Trish felt no rush of excitement at this promising new lead. Instead, all the strength in her body seemed to be drawn downward. With her aunt and her father as suspects, she didn't foresee much possibility of a happy outcome.

With the necessary search warrants already on his desk, Carter ordered the other two deputies to go together to Hank and Lamar Valliere's homes, Noah Franklin's and Grey's to search for the shirt missing this button. Carter looked up at her. "Trish, you and I will take care of searching your aunt's house."

Filled with heavy foreboding, Trish could barely nod her agreement.

Carter handed out the warrants.

Soon, with Trish in the Jeep beside him, Carter was parking in the alley behind her aunt's bungalow. On the way there, she'd decided that Carter had brought her along to Harriet's for a couple of reasons. First, she sensed that Carter didn't think Harriet had done more than let one of the three men use her vehicle. And second, Harriet might prefer to have Trish there while the sheriff did the actual searching. Or perhaps Carter thought that Trish could deal best with Harriet's complaints about the search and keep her out of the sheriff's way. Whatever the reason, here they were.

Harriet answered the door and greeted them with indignation and loud complaints. But since they were armed with a warrant, she had no choice but to let them in.

At Carter's order, Trish asked her aunt to sit down at her kitchen table while Carter searched. Harriet sat with her lips pressed together and her arms folded defiantly. Trish sighed inwardly and tried not to take her aunt's resentment personally. *All in a day's work.* Once again, returning to the Madison Police Department began to seem like a good idea. She wouldn't be a part of this if she'd stayed there.

Minutes passed. Trish could hear Carter rifling through

drawers, scraping hangers in closets while her aunt stared a hole in Trish's forehead. Then Carter appeared in the kitchen. "Where do you do your laundry?"

Harriet grimaced, but barked, "Basement."

Carter hurried down the steps.

"I can't believe you're working against your own family," Harriet hissed.

"I can't believe my own family would break the law," Trish retorted, fed up.

Harriet's face reddened at this and then she wouldn't look Trish in the eye. "Who's proven we broke the law?"

Carter came up the basement stairs. "Mrs. Franklin, I'm taking this shirt as evidence—"

"What?" Harriet sprang to her feet. "You can't take—"

"This shirt is missing a button and it appears to match a button found at the crime scene," Carter said with a glance toward Trish.

Trish felt the blood drain from her face. She'd never felt that before. She felt clammy and a little faint. *My aunt is the one responsible for the hit-and-runs? No.*

"That doesn't prove a thing," Harriet blustered. "I have every right to be on my own property. It proves nothing."

"The button was found *inside* the gray sedan that you told us—when we've questioned you repeatedly—you haven't been in or driven for years."

"How can you prove that that's even my shirt?" Harriet countered.

"A DNA test will be able to prove whether you've worn this shirt or not."

Harriet stood with her mouth open.

"I think you'd better get your purse and come with us," Carter said, taking another step forward.

"I'm not going anywhere with you."

"I'm afraid I can compel you, Mrs. Franklin," Carter said, a deep frown creasing his forehead.

"He can," Trish muttered, trying to pull herself together.

"I'm not going—" Harriet turned to reach for her phone.

"Mrs. Franklin, you can call your lawyer from my office," Carter said, taking the receiver from her.

Trish watched in horror as her aunt began to pummel Carter with her balled fists. Trish jumped up. Carter grabbed her aunt's wrists. "Mrs. Franklin, I don't want to hurt you. And I'd prefer not to have to use the cuffs."

"I haven't done anything wrong!" Harriet shouted.

Trish recognized the shrill tone of dawning hysteria. She drew closer to her aunt's side. "Auntie, please don't resist. Calm yourself." She stroked her aunt's shoulder and murmured more calming phrases. "Come with us and you can call your lawyer as soon as the sheriff compares this shirt with the evidence. It might not even match and you'll be upsetting yourself all for nothing."

Trish's words finally appeared to work. Harriet stopped struggling and let Trish help her with her coat. The three of them left for the sheriff's department.

In his office in front of Trish and another deputy, Carter matched the button and cloth fragment to the shirt from Aunt Harriet's hamper. He looked up at Trish. "I think you better come with me to face your aunt."

Wordlessly, Trish went into the interrogation room and confronted Harriet. This time Harriet reacted with shock. Her face paled and beads of perspiration dotted her forehead. "I think I'm going to pass out."

Trish hurried over and helped her aunt lower her head to her knees. Trish again stroked her aunt's back and murmured encouragement. In a few moments, her aunt was able to sit up again.

"Mrs. Franklin," Carter said, "you can call your lawyer now. Come to my office. Then we'll book you."

Moving like a robot, Harriet followed the sheriff's instructions. She clung to Trish, who looked up the number for her aunt and then dialed Harriet's lawyer for her. Her aunt tried to speak to the man, but couldn't. She handed the receiver to Trish and mumbled, "Please."

Trish took the receiver and quickly explained the situation. Then she hung up. "He'll come soon and talk over bail and everything with you."

Both Carter and Trish had to help her aunt up from the chair. Trish stayed at her aunt's side throughout the process of being booked. And then Trish helped her aunt back to the interrogation room. The sheriff hadn't wanted to upset Harriet further by putting her in the holding cell.

Carter walked out of the room. Trish touched her aunt's shoulder. "Do you want me to stay?"

Harriet nodded and then whispered, "I never meant to hurt anybody."

Trish's heart contracted at this near admission of guilt. She sat down beside her aunt and put her arm around her. To Trish, the past half hour had been a bad dream, a bad dream where she was forced to watch horrible events unfold, frozen to the spot when she should have been running for her life. *Dear Lord, my aunt—I can't believe it. I don't want to believe it.*

ON THE WAY HOME FROM a painting job, Grey stopped by the convenience store to pick up a gallon of milk. His shirtsleeves were rolled up. The past few days had continued to be warm, more Indian summer days. Eddie looked up from behind the counter and called to him, "Hey, buddy, you won't believe what I just heard."

"What's that?" Grey asked, opening the chilled glass dairy case and selecting the two percent milk his aunt preferred.

"They've arrested Trish's aunt for the hit-and-runs."

The plastic gallon of milk nearly slipped from Grey's hand. "Jake's widow?"

"Yeah, hard to believe, isn't it?"

Grey walked to the counter. "Yes, that's awful."

"Arrested her and everything."

Grey just stood there gawking at Eddie, trying to make sense of it. "What was she thinking?"

Eddie shrugged. "Getting back at you, man. You'd think that after seven years people would get over things. I mean, seven years."

Grey nodded. "Some people just can't let go...I guess." He handed Eddie a five and then pocketed his change.

"I guess that means all the excitement is over now." Eddie gave him a twisted smile.

Grey shook his head, as if trying to make this fit into his brain. "I never expected it to be her."

"Yeah, my bet was on Noah or Lamar. It's a funny world."

"I guess." Was this the end of it? Would everything calm down now? He'd thought the sheriff arresting someone would bring relief. It hadn't. Just a feeling of uncertainty, of confusion. Trish's face flickered in his mind. How was she taking this? Grey turned to leave and then stopped. "Why don't you come over for supper some night this week?"

"I'll try. But I'm sort of trying to strike something up with a new waitress in town. She comes into Bugsy's most every evening after work and I don't want any other guy to make a move while I'm away. Know what I mean?"

Grey left with a wave. The news of the arrest had left him feeling hollow but leaden, simultaneously empty and heavy. Outside, he was just about to get into the Chrysler when a black truck careened in off the highway. It jerked to a halt in front of the Chrysler, blocking Grey.

Lamar and Hank climbed out of the truck. Hank had a rifle in hand.

Grey shoved the milk into the Chrysler and backed away from the two men, his hands raised. The presence of the rifle raised his conflict with the Vallieres to a new chilling level.

"We're going to settle everything here and now," Hank yelled. "We know you're the one the sheriff should have arrested today!"

"Yeah, it's pretty smart of you to make up to that Franklin girl, one of the deputies investigating this," Lamar joined in.

"But that's not going to help you," Hank continued as the two of them circled Grey. "Here and now. Once and for all, we're going to take revenge for Darleen."

Grey kept his back to the Chrysler and shifted, keeping an eye on both men. "So, two against one," he said, trying to figure a way out of this. "And I'm unarmed. Are you planning on shooting me here in cold blood?"

"No, Lamar is going to beat the stuffing out of you," Hank sneered. "I'm just going to make sure no one interferes."

With a baseball bat in hand, Eddie rushed out the door toward the three of them, shouting, "Get out of here! I just called 911! Scram! Or you'll wish you had!"

Lamar halted but made no move to run. And Hank lifted the rifle to his shoulder.

"Go back inside, Eddie," Grey ordered, suddenly afraid that Hank might actually pull the trigger. "I don't want you to get hurt."

"I'm not going anywhere," Eddie said, his voice rich with suppressed excitement. "I've been waiting years to see Lamar's backside kicked."

Another truck rattled into view. With a sinking heart, Grey recognized it as Noah Franklin's. *Hail, hail, the gang's all here.*

Chapter 12

A baseball bat, a rifle, and now Noah was charging out of his truck, armed with a shotgun. Sanity was slipping away. Grey couldn't think. His mind had locked up like a corrupted computer file. One thought gleamed clearly. He couldn't let Eddie take another hit meant for him. And then he recalled that Eddie had alerted the sheriff. Help should be on the way. But could he keep things from boiling over till it arrived?

"We should have done this two months ago!" Noah declared. "If we'd run him out of town then, none of this would have happened and Jake's widow wouldn't be sitting in jail now."

His hands still above his head, Grey tried to keep his eyes on all three who now circled him like a pack of dogs, yapping around wounded prey. *God, send help soon.*

"You're the one who ought to be run out of town!" Eddie retorted. "You're sick, old man! You ought to be put in a home!"

"Worthless punk!" Noah leaped forward. Before Eddie could swing the bat, Noah rammed the steel barrel of the shotgun into Eddie's midsection. Eddie yelped and then doubled up, groaning. Grey wanted to go to Eddie's aid. But that would only draw all three—Lamar, Hank and Noah—toward his friend. Grey moved sideways, away from Eddie who'd dropped down onto one knee, moaning.

"Haven't the three of you learned anything from what's just happened to Harriet Franklin today?" Grey kept his voice even, not showing any fear or any disdain that might trigger more anger. He'd learned this from watching prison guards defuse jail fights. "You're all so busy trying to take revenge on me that you're putting yourselves over the line. You're breaking the law. Is making trouble for me worth going to jail?"

"Yes!" Lamar lunged forward, swinging his fist as he came.

Grey dodged the blow.

Off balance, Lamar caught himself and tried and missed again.

Noah and Hank edged forward, each one covering Grey with their weapons. Grey began praying for help to arrive. Soon. "I'm not fighting you, Lamar," Grey declared, playing for time, for sanity to return. "This is three against one. I'm unarmed and no one in Winfield is going to think you did right."

With his fists raised, Lamar looked as if he weren't paying any attention. But he didn't swing again, just continued to move in on Grey's space.

"And you know it," Grey finished. In spite of the cool autumn air, sweat popped out on his forehead, beaded and trickled down the sides of his face.

Lamar continued to spar. Grey kept his hands in the air and evaded Lamar as he continued to crowd in on Grey.

Then the marvelous sound of sirens ripped through the air. From both directions, three sheriff's vehicles barreled in off the highway.

"Thank you, God!" Grey said silently and let his arms fall to his sides.

Lamar turned and pelted back to his black pickup.

"Yeah!" Eddie shouted, even though it sounded as if it pained him to speak. "Now you're in for it! Loser!"

Hank and Noah whirled around, glaring. But made no move to run. Two of the sheriff's vehicles blocked Noah's and Lamar's trucks. Nowhere to run. Nowhere to hide.

Grey hurried to Eddie and knelt beside him. "Are you okay, buddy?"

Eddie tried to grin. "Never...been rammed with shotgun before," Eddie wheezed. "I don't...recommend it."

Grey helped Eddie to rise and sit down sideways in the open Chrysler.

———

WITH THEIR SIDEARMS DRAWN, the sheriff and three deputies, including Trish, approached the men. The sheriff ordered, "Franklin, Valliere, lay that rifle and shotgun down on the ground and put your hands on your heads!"

Trembling, Trish didn't let dismay stop her. *I'm holding a gun on my father.*

Neither Hank nor Noah moved to obey. They stood their ground, their weapons held waist-high.

"Lay down your weapons! Now! Don't make us shoot!" Carter ordered.

The deputies raised their weapons, prepared.

As she aimed her Glock, Trish's heart had never beaten so fast. It felt as if it might come up her throat. The 911 call hadn't mentioned her father. If it had, Carter probably wouldn't have ordered her along. Should she say something to her father? No. She'd only pour lighter fluid on her father's flaming out-of-control rage.

"We don't want any trouble with the law," Hank finally said and squatting, laid his rifle on the pavement in front of him.

Then he turned to Noah. "Lay it down. We don't have a choice."

Her father glared into Trish's eyes. Then he spat on the ground toward her.

She made no sign that she saw what he'd done. Her stomach swayed within her in a sickening rhythm. This is a nightmare, Lord. Don't let it get worse. I don't want to witness my father brought down by another deputy.

"Mr. Franklin!" Carter shouted. "This is your last chance. Lay down your shotgun! Or my deputies will shoot."

At the last possible second, her father shouted a curse and lowered his shotgun to the ground.

Trish swallowed down her heart. She tried to catch her breath.

Carter glanced her way. "Go to Eddie and help him. See if he needs the EMTs." Then he and the two other deputies moved to arrest and handcuff Lamar, Hank and Noah.

Finally, Trish made her way to Eddie. At the open door of the Chrysler, Trish faced Grey over Eddie's head; everything inside her clamored for her to go to him and pull him close. Instead she asked, "How badly are you hurt, Eddie?"

"Your dad rammed me with his shotgun. It's probably going to be one nasty bruise." Eddie tried to chuckle but stopped as if that hurt too much.

"Let's get him up and into the sheriff's Jeep," she said. With Grey's help, she got Eddie up and headed toward the Jeep.

"Hey," Eddie said, halting the three of them. "I can't just go off and leave the convenience store unattended. I gotta go back in and finish my shift. If I screw up again, Ollie said he'd fire me."

"Eddie," Grey countered, "you're hurt."

"Not that bad. I'm not bleeding. I can't...just leave, man. Can't lose my job."

Trish called to the sheriff, who was leading her father toward his vehicle. "We need to call Ollie and tell him what's happened. Eddie says he can't leave the convenience store unattended."

"Okay," the sheriff replied. "Get Ollie on your cell phone and ask him to come here now. I'm sure everything that just went down has been recorded from the security system Ollie put in to record people who drive off without paying."

"Great," Eddie said, still clutching his midsection. "These three need to be behind bars."

Noah called Eddie a nasty name. Carter made no response to this and after patting her handcuffed father down, he guided him into the back of his Jeep, behind the grill, and shut the door.

Trish stared at the sight. Her father being taken in to be booked for attempted assault.

Carter turned to Grey. "I need to get these three in and start booking them. But I'll need you to come in as soon as possible for a statement, and to press assault charges against them. And we need Eddie's statement, too."

"I don't know." Grey looked abashed.

"Don't worry about what my family thinks," Trish said, not looking toward Grey. "My father needs a dose of reality before he goes too far and really hurts someone. You'd be doing him a favor." Could dementia be part of her father's problem? But legally she couldn't ask to see her father's medical records. If her father didn't get back to reality soon, he might have to be declared incompetent for his own protection and that of others. And that would kill him. Did he even guess at how much trouble he was in? From his defiant glare, she thought no.

Carter nodded. "She's right. Her father's behavior is...deteriorating." Carter lowered his voice. "He needs help before he gets into real trouble, before he really hurts someone."

Not waiting to hear Grey's reply, Trish walked Eddie slowly toward the convenience store. If the sheriff didn't call what had just taken place "real trouble," she sure did.

"WHAT NEXT?" WERE THE words that popped into Trish's mind. Only yesterday, her father, Lamar and Hank had all been booked into the county jail. This morning, Trish stood in the silent courtroom where just a few weeks ago, she'd watched Rae-Jean being sentenced. Now she waited for her father's arraignment on assault. She wished she could be anywhere but here. But this was what a good daughter had to do.

She wondered if the lawyer had had any luck with Noah. He'd been resisting the lawyer and insisting that he would plead "guilty." That would lead to dire legal consequences. *Lord, help my father see reason. This is bad enough without making it worse for himself.*

Chaney, Penny and Florence stood on one side of Trish. And on the other was Aunt Harriet, who couldn't seem to stop crying. Was she weeping for herself or Noah? *What a way to spend a day off duty,* Trish thought, forced to watch her elders self-destruct.

The bailiff called out, "All rise."

The sparsely populated courtroom shuffled to its feet. Trish watched the black-robed judge take his seat and the proceedings began. She'd been in this courtroom many times. Watching Rae-Jean's sentencing had been rough enough. But today she couldn't take her eyes off her orange-clad father.

An image from her childhood taunted her. A younger, grinning Noah was baiting her hook as they fished off the pier. Her brothers around them jeered, like the boys they were, that she must learn to bait her own hooks. Her father had only chuckled and ruffled her bangs. Where had that man gone?

First Lamar, then Hank and finally Noah replied to the

judge when he asked them for their plea. To her relief, all three pled, "Not guilty." Bail was set and the three were led out. The court continued with another case.

Immense relief filled Trish as her family filed out of the courtroom. Then, out in the hallway, Aunt Harriet broke down completely, sobbing and looking faint. Trish, Penny and Florence all tried to comfort her. But she appeared to be beyond their feeble attempts.

Penny, who was a part-time nurse, nudged Harriet onto a stalwart oak bench in the hallway and took her sobbing aunt's pulse. "We should take her to the ER. Her pulse is twice what it should be," Penny murmured.

"I've done something stupid. I need...to talk to the...sheriff," Harriet gasped, pressing her hand against her heart. "My chest hurts."

That phrase galvanized them. Though straining, Chaney managed to lift Harriet and carry her out to his pickup. Then in their separate vehicles, they all raced for the hospital. Trish couldn't remember a time when they'd had to take so many members of her family into the ER before. And in such a short span of time. It hadn't been this bad when her brothers were playing high school football in the same season.

At the ER, Chaney left them. He had to go home to sleep so he could work that evening and Penny had to go home and get dressed to come back to the hospital to work at one. So Florence sat beside Trish on the stiff chairs while Harriet was admitted to a room for observation. Harriet's words kept going around and around in Trish's mind. What had her aunt been thinking, doing?

Florence recalled an appointment and had to leave. Finally, Trish alone entered her aunt's semiprivate room. "Auntie, is there anything you need from home?"

"I need...to talk to the sheriff." Harriet's voice was thin and frightened.

"I don't think you should do that without your lawyer present," Trish cautioned.

"I've done a stupid thing, more than one stupid thing. And I need to make a clean breast of everything—"

"Stop. Don't tell me anything about the case pending against you." Trish almost put her hands over her ears. "I'm an officer of the court and I must report anything you tell me. And I can and will have to testify against you in court about anything you might tell me."

"I—don't—care." Harriet spaced out her words for emphasis. "This has gone too far and I started it all." She drew in a shaky breath. "But I don't know who's doing it now. I have to tell the sheriff—" The monitor Harriet was hooked to began beeping a loud warning. A nurse rushed in, waving Trish out of the room. Then a doctor charged past Trish.

Harriet called weakly after Trish. "I did the first two hit-and-runs. But just those two!"

And then Harriet was shushed by the nurse. The doctor barked at Trish. "I think you'd better leave. You're agitating her."

His words ringing in her ears, Trish escaped down the hall to the elevator. On the first floor, she hurried outside and punched in the sheriff's number on her cell phone. Her aunt's words ricocheted in her mind. Aunt Harriet was guilty. But only of the first two? Who had taken over for her then?

THE WINFIELD GOSSIP grapevine hadn't failed him. He'd heard the news about Harriet's confession the next morning. Harriet had confessed to the first two hit-and-runs but was denying that she'd done the third and fourth. Public opinion was split on whether she was telling the truth or not. Well, he knew she was telling the truth. *But I'm not talking.*

The incident at Ollie's had been the last straw. He'd take care of Grey before the weekend. He couldn't go through much more. It had to end. And he'd end it in such a way that Grey would be charged and convicted of the fifth and final hit-and-run.

I have everything to lose—if the whole truth ever comes out. And his nerves couldn't take much more. This was a case of self-defense. It was him or Grey. And he'd make sure it was Grey.

———

THAT AFTERNOON TRISH drove up the bumpy lane to Elsie's house. She'd been on her way home, but then she'd seen the new white sign on Elsie's property. And suddenly she knew how Eddie had felt the day before yesterday when her father rammed him with the shotgun. No, it couldn't be true. She wouldn't let it be true.

She got out and heard the unmistakable scraping of a rake nearby. Hurrying around to the backyard, she saw Grey raking up the thick layer of bronzed, crinkled leaves. Grey's muscles moved under his sleeveless T-shirt as he stretched out the rake and brought it back. Sunlight picked up the silver at his temples. And cast his angular features into shadow and light. She closed her eyes.

It was as if someone had flipped on a switch inside her. Suddenly she was alive, more alive than she'd ever dreamed of being. Previously when Grey had kissed her, she'd only sampled a foretaste of this exquisite sensitivity. This was more, much more than she'd ever experienced before. *Grey, I'm in love with you.*

She walked up to him and touched his shoulder. He swung around, looking startled. "I didn't hear you coming."

There was so much she wanted to say to him, but the emotions rolling, crashing through her made her mute. Once again, she rested her head against his chest, hearing his heart beat under her ear. She could smell the trace of his honest sweat, mingled with the scent of the fabric softener Elsie used. "Grey," she murmured and pressed her face against his soft T-shirt. Pure joy flowed through her. This wasn't mere attraction. If this wasn't love, what else could it be?

———

NO. DON'T, TRISH. Letting the rake fall, Grey took hold of Trish's slender shoulders. He knew he should set her away from him. But he first had to draw up all his defenses. And with her so close, touching him, he found that this was almost impossible. Her auburn hair tickled his nose. He couldn't stop himself. He brushed his cheek against the vibrant silken strands. He tightened his grip, tucking her even closer to him. *I shouldn't be doing this. Why can't I push her away?*

Finally, sanity returned. He set her away from him and held her there, his hands on her upper arms. "Trish, no."

She looked up at him, feeling dazed. Didn't he feel it, too? "Yes." She tried to break his hold and return to his chest.

He held her arms firmly but gently within his large hands. "Trish, you must have seen the For Sale sign. We're leaving Winfield. For good. For everyone's good."

"No," she said, rejecting this. "You can't."

"I must," he said, leaning down and speaking close to her face. "Elsie and I talked it over last night. My presence here has stirred up things that should have been left to rest. After that scene at Ollie's, I can't take any more."

"No. I love you, Grey. You can't leave me, leave us."

"No." Turning his face away, he tried not to let her see how much it cut him to speak these words to her. But he had to make her understand. "You shouldn't say that, Trish. I'm leaving. Elsie has put her house up for sale. The sign on the road just went up. I have a few jobs here to finish and then we're leaving Winfield for good."

Her spine stiffened. *This isn't the Middle Ages, Grey. I'm a free agent.* "Then I'll leave Winfield, too. I only came back here from Madison to take care of my dad. And we both know that he won't even let me on his property now—not after yesterday."

"I'm sorry about that. If I hadn't returned here, you and your dad would still—"

"That's not true." She tried to move closer but he held her away. "Dad didn't want me here. He's been as rude as he can be to me. And that started *way* before you came home so don't take that blame on yourself. I can't let my father's irrational behavior ruin my life, ruin our love." Her voice cracked on the final word. *You can't stop me from loving you.*

Grey wouldn't meet Trish's eyes. Where did she get the courage to make these declarations? Her daring humbled him, frightened him for her. He longed to kiss her for her bravery. But instead, he tightened his hold. He resisted both equally, her effort to push nearer to him again and his own need to hold her close. "Trish, it's not just your dad. I'm an ex-con on early release. You're a law officer. The two don't go together."

She tossed her head as if shaking off his comment. "I don't *have* to be a law officer. I can do something else where your..." Her voice trailed off.

"Where my being a felon won't affect you?" He completed her statement. "But my being a felon will affect me all my life and if we were together...it would affect you, too. I can't change that, Trish. And I won't inflict it on you."

"I don't care." She looked up at him, her chin lifted in defiance. "I love you and I don't care. I know that you are a different man now than—"

He squeezed her arms. "Stop it. I'm still an alcoholic—"

"You're not drinking anymore. What has that—"

"It has everything to do with...with anyone I become...involved with. I could crack at any time and start drinking again. And then I'd be put back behind bars." He lowered his face so that he was eye to eye with her.

"You won't crack." Their relationship was already difficult. Why was he trying to make it impossible? "If you love me and I love you, you won't fall off the wagon."

He released her arms. "You can't say that. Do you know how hard it is for me to drive past Bugsy's and not go in? Do you have any idea how hard it is for me to walk into Ollie's and only buy milk? Alcohol still calls to me, still tempts me. I can't and won't deny that." He took a step back from her.

Trish couldn't believe he was being this stubborn. Didn't he know how rare love was in this hard world? "There is nothing between us that can't be worked out. Do you think I fall in love every day? I've never been in love before. You are a fine man. And anyone who knows you knows that. Why won't you admit it?"

"Because seven years ago I made the flawed decision to drive drunk and I killed two people. Two people died because of my alcohol abuse. Nothing can ever change that. Nothing." He folded his arms. *Give it up, Trish.*

I'm not giving up, Grey. "I don't know about Darleen, but my uncle Jake would have forgiven you. He looked like my dad but he wasn't *like* my dad. His heart never got cold and brittle. He never loved being miserable and trying to make others as miserable as he was. You can't change what happened seven years ago, but no one alive can live a sinless life. And your sin is no greater than any other person's sin. All sin is equal in God's eyes. I'm a sinner, too."

He took another step back from her. "It's not the same."

"Are you calling God a liar?" she demanded, feeling her face flush. "He says this is so. 'For by grace are you saved through faith that is not of yourselves. It is a gift of God not works lest any man should boast.'"

Grey wanted to shake her. This wasn't about God, but about people and their prejudices. "God sees it that way. But people don't. And we live in a world of people. What if we got married and somehow it came out that I was a convicted felon, what would it do to you, to...our kids?"

That he had already carried his guilt to the next generation ignited her temper. "And so no one can have a wife and kids if they made a bad decision?" She jabbed his chest with her index finger. "Jesus died on the cross for the forgiveness of our sins. If you keep holding on to your guilt, it's like you're trying to climb up and join Him. It's not right. It's not God's will. And He didn't stay on the cross. He died once for all and rose again. All your sins, past, present and future were forgiven the day you accepted Christ as your savior. Holding on to this guilt is...it's just wrong. You can't let the prejudice of others do that to you, to us."

He took another step back, away from her hand. "I can't change how I feel."

"Neither can I. I love you, Grey Lawson. And nothing, nothing will ever change my mind." She glared at him. Her hands itched to grab his shoulders and shake him until he saw sense.

"No. Trish, don't love me. I'm leaving. Elsie's house is up for sale—we're moving. I've already made an appointment to see my parole officer and notify him that I will be changing addresses. Pastor Ray said he'll look around for a job for me down in Oneida County where he pastored another church. It's over, Trish. I'm leaving. It's best for both of us and that's final."

Then she did seize his arms and attempted to shake him. "I'm not through with you, Grey. Get that through your head. And there are a lot of people who won't be happy to see you leave." She turned away, holding in the rest of the hot furious words that wanted to spill out. She had to keep her cool. "Carter and I will solve this case and then life can settle down, so you can think straight." She walked away, loving him, wanting to pound sense into him. If only she could open his skull and excise all the crippling guilt he carried.

"I am thinking straight," he called after her. "You're not."

She cast him a determined look and got into her Jeep and drove off. I pity the person who's responsible for the last two games of chicken. When I get hold of them...

Remembering that she was a Christian and supposed to forgive, she didn't finish that sentence. But she would take great satisfaction when she snapped the cuffs on—whoever it was. *Who is it, Lord? I need to find out before it's too late.*

THE NEXT EVENING AT DUSK, damp fog rolled in once again, a thick fog which filled him with courage. Tonight was the night. He'd take care of Grey once and for all tonight. And then he would be able to sleep again.

Sitting in his pickup, he pulled the cell phone he'd lifted from some drunk at Bugsy's last night and punched in Noah Franklin's number. The old coot answered with a gruff, "Yeah."

"If you want to catch Lawson in the act, drive slowly east down Cross-cut Road. Now." He hung up, grinning, and drove toward County N where Grey was finishing up a handyman job. Everything would go right this time. Noah Franklin would be silenced for good. And Grey would be charged with the hit-and-runs, another vehicular homicide and go back to prison and never get out again. *And I'll be home free for good.*

Parking his truck in the shelter of a group of thick fir trees just off the road, he then walked up the drive, past Grey's

Chrysler and up the outside staircase to the house Grey was working on. When he went in, he called out, "Grey, hey it's me!"

Grey turned from where he was running water, cleaning up his paint roller at the sink. "Hey, Eddie, what brings you here?"

"I was just driving past and my truck just stopped and I can't get it to turn over. Could you come out and jump me? I think it's my battery. I need a new one. And maybe a new air filter."

"Sure."

A feather of guilt brushed Eddie's conscience. But he ignored it. He'd been ignoring his conscience for a long time. Only Grey made him feel guilty. And Grey would be gone before long. And for good. If Grey didn't die in the process of killing Noah in a head-on collision, he'd still be sent back to jail for the attempt. No one would believe Grey if he said he hadn't been drinking and driving. No one. Not even that pretty redheaded cop.

The thickening fog wrapped itself around them. Eddie walked next to Grey to the Chrysler and got in on the passenger side. Then Grey backed them down the drive to the road. "Where's your vehicle?"

"Over there." Eddie pointed through the mist to where his truck was parked.

Grey gave him a funny look, but parked his Chrysler nose to nose with Eddie's truck. Grey got out and opened the creaky trunk and walked around with the red and black jumper cables in hand. Eddie had already opened the hood of his truck. Grey bent over the engine to attach the cables. Eddie struck the back of Grey's head with a wrench he'd been holding at his side. Grey dropped to the ground—out cold. After slamming down the hood, Eddie pulled on gloves and returned the cables to the Chrysler trunk. And then from his vehicle, he retrieved and tossed a glossy black helmet onto the front seat.

Straining, he half lifted, half dragged Grey into the driver's side seat, and shoved him behind the wheel of the Chrysler. He seat-belted Grey in, glad that the older car had the shoulder-strap-style belt, which would hold Grey up in front of the wheel. Eddie got in and sliding close to Grey on the bench seat, started the Chrysler from Grey's right side. He put the cell phone in Grey's limp right hand so that it would have his prints on it. And then he leaned down and wrapped a piece of twine tightly around Grey's foot, binding it to the pedal. He'd press down on top of Grey's foot so it would be Grey's footprint alone on the gas pedal. He'd thought this through so many times. Nothing must be wrong this time.

After impact, he'd hurry back to the Chrysler, whisk the twine off and then escape into the woods. He'd be able to walk through the heavily wooded areas back to his truck without anyone being the wiser. *So far, so good.*

Then he pulled a small bottle of whiskey out of his pocket and poured some into Grey's mouth, tilting his head back, hoping some would leak down Grey's throat. Eddie then poured the rest of the booze onto Grey's shirt. As the odor of the liquor filled the car, he grinned.

Finally, he pulled on the black biking helmet he'd stolen from a Harley outside Bugsy's last night. This was almost too easy. When they find his body, it will reek of whiskey. And I'll confess that he bought the bottle from me at Ollie's—even though I tried to talk him out of it.

With difficulty, Eddie worked the steering wheel with one hand and then stretched to fit his left foot over Grey's on the gas pedal. Then backing up onto the road, Eddie drove into the wonderfully thick fog and headed fast toward Cross-cut, a conveniently long east-west road. Noah Franklin should be coming right toward them from his place.

Reaching Cross-cut, Eddie drove slowly, encumbered by Grey's unconscious form leaning against him. Now all he had to do was drive down the middle of the road until Noah Franklin's truck appeared. The handy fog would conceal him as he went about what he had to do.

He heard it then—Noah's truck's distinctive tinny rattle. Pulling the helmet strap tight, he shoved open the passenger side door, so he could jump at the last minute—before impact. He steered to the middle of the road, his heart thumping. He pressed the gas pedal down hard. *Just a little farther, a little farther and all my problems will be over. I'll be free again.*

Chapter 13

Driving east on Cross-cut through the heavy fog, Trish could still hear her father's truck ahead of her. And speeding up, she saw his red taillights glowing through the mist. Where was he headed so slowly as if he were looking for someone?

After work, she'd headed to Noah's place to have it out with him about Grey. But he'd been just driving away. He'd seen her but had ignored her waving and honking for him to pull over. It had made her so mad that she'd chased him. *You're not getting away with stonewalling anymore, Dad. Afterward, we may not be on speaking terms—*

Then she heard it—the familiar sound of Elsie's Chrysler. And it sounded as if it was going really fast. And then it all happened before her eyes.

Ahead within the thinning mist, she glimpsed the Chrysler barreling down the center line, aiming for her father's truck. She gasped. Its passenger's side door was open. She screamed. Her father's bald tires squealed, screeched. But in vain. A man leaped out the door of the Chrysler.

An explosion of metal... Bang!

She swerved to miss the accident. But the man on the road!

He was right in her path. She couldn't stop in time! Skidding. She twisted her wheel to miss him. But she was out of control and trapped between the vehicles and tree-lined shoulder. She hit him. With a sickening thump, he landed on her hood. Her SUV finally ended its skid. For a few seconds, she clutched the steering wheel, gasping for air.

Then she snapped open her cell phone and speed-dialed. "Dispatch, this is Trish. I've just been involved in a two-vehicle collision on Cross-cut near Highway 57. I'm sure there will be someone injured." She cut off before the dispatcher could demand any more information. She yanked the first aid kit from under her dash.

She went first to the man facedown on her hood. She felt for a pulse and then as gently as she could, she turned his face toward her. Eddie? It was Eddie? Why would Eddie be wearing a biker helmet and jumping out of Elsie's Chrysler? His face was bleeding. She ran her hands over his limp body, trying to find any other obvious injuries. Then she saw it.

A trail of blood was coming from his midsection and flowing meagerly down the hood of her SUV, dripping onto the ground. She considered moving him, but she might make him bleed more. The pressure of his body might be acting as a pressure bandage. The blood was flowing, not pulsing or pouring. Better not to move him and possibly make matters worse.

Praying the ambulance would get there soon, she turned to the other two vehicles. It had been a nearly perfect head-on collision. But the Chrysler had swerved to the left. With its right headlight, it had plowed into her dad's old truck, catching it near its right headlight. The two vehicles were tangled together in a mesh of grills and crumpled hoods.

Partially concealed by an airbag, Grey was slumped behind the wheel of the Chrysler. What was going on? Everything she'd seen jumbled up in her mind into a tangle just like the one before her. Her father had been driving slowly but steadily down Cross-cut with her behind him. Grey had been driving the Chrysler down the center line at her father? And Eddie had jumped from the Chrysler? She didn't want to work it all out right now. The implications, the vibrations of what this all meant threatened to overpower her.

She pushed them aside. She was a first-responder. She had accident victims to help. She went to her father first. He was older, in frailer health and without an airbag. She couldn't pry open the crumpled driver's side door. So she hurried around to the other side and crawled in.

She felt her father's carotid pulse and his heart was beating. He was breathing, shallow but breathing. Of course, he hadn't been wearing his seat belt. He'd been driving without one for sixty years, right? She heard his voice as if he'd just repeated the words. She swallowed to keep tears at bay. Worse yet, the cab of the pickup had accordioned. His chest was compressed against the steering wheel. His forehead was bleeding. "Dad," she said. "Dad, it's me, Trish. Can you hear me?"

No reply.

He was also bleeding into the front of his shirt. Probably damage from some cracked and broken ribs. Again, she considered moving him. But he was wedged in and she couldn't get him out alone, not safely. She dragged in a ragged breath and headed over to see how bad Grey was.

The Chrysler had been lifted up by the pickup's front bumper. But the passenger side had taken the brunt of the collision. And the ancient airbag had deployed. She hadn't thought the old car had an airbag. So Grey had been protected from the impact. He was slumped back against the headrest and driver's seat. She felt his pulse. His heart was beating and he was breathing. She noted a trace of blood on the seat behind his head.

Then she saw it. Grey's foot had been tied with twine to the accelerator. Her mind froze as she stared at it.

Finally, she heard the blessed sound of sirens. In the past few minutes, she'd aged a decade.

Within a short time, she was standing in the damp mist, answering Carter's questions about her description of what she'd witnessed and watching the other deputies swarm around the collision. Then the ambulances screeched to a halt nearby. The EMTs had to use the Jaws of Life to cut her father free. Trish wrapped her arms around herself to keep from screaming at them. Then the three accident victims were rushed off to the ER.

When Carter asked one of the other deputies to drive her home in her SUV, Trish came out of her shock. "I can drive," she muttered. She took another deep breath. "I can drive," she said in a more normal voice.

Carter studied her by the headlight glow from a nearby Jeep. "You don't look good. Come on. Someone will drive you home."

She touched his sleeve. "I'm going to Elsie's to tell her about this and then I'll drive her to Ashford to be with Grey."

Carter squeezed her shoulder. "Wait, I'm calling your brother Andy. He should be with you. And with your father."

She turned away. "Tell him to meet me at Elsie's."

"Okay, if you're sure." He stopped her with a touch on her shoulder and lowered his voice. "And you don't have any idea why Eddie was wearing a helmet and jumping from the Chrysler? Or why Grey's foot was tied to the accelerator?"

She turned back and focused on Carter, wrapped in the dreary fog. "I wish I could confess to imagining it."

"All of it gives me ideas," Carter said. "Nasty, twisted ones."

"Me, too." She walked toward her SUV, which had settled onto the shoulder. It had just missed hitting a lodgepole pine.

She waved and walked away toward her fog-shrouded vehicle. But now she'd glimpsed the truth about Grey and Eddie, seen through the mist of lies, through the impenetrable fog that had obscured the truth for over seven years.

⊏⊐

LATER, AS MUCH OF HER family as could come at this late hour, Andy, Penny, Elsie and Trish sat in the surgical waiting area. Both Noah and Eddie had suffered internal injuries from the accident. Grey had suffered bruised ribs, bruising from both seat belt and airbag, and shock. He'd also sustained a blow to the back of his head but wasn't concussed. He was sedated and was being kept for observation overnight. Trish and Elsie had visited his room, but left him since they wouldn't be able to speak to him until morning.

"I still can't believe this," Andy muttered.

"I saw it happen right in front of me and I can't, either," Trish replied.

"Why would Eddie do that?" Penny asked again.

Trish had just finished putting it all together. But she couldn't let anything slip. She needed to talk to the sheriff and soon. Elsie was sitting beside her, waiting for Trish to drive her home. She didn't want to be the one to tell Elsie what it all meant.

The surgeon in green scrubs walked down the hall to them. "Are you the Franklin family?"

Andy rose first. "Yes. How is our father?"

"Noah faces a long recovery time. His heart is weak and he's suffered severe internal bleeding. We think we have it stopped now. But he'll be in the ICU for at least three days, maybe longer."

After everything that had happened this evening, Trish already felt as if the whole world had been dropped on top of her. Her father's shaky condition was the final straw. Her knees weakened. She barely made a nod at the surgeon's words and then sat back down. *Lord, I haven't been much help to my dad.*

"You should all go home," the surgeon said. "Your father is sedated and won't be talking to anyone until tomorrow."

Andy nodded to all of them and they turned to leave.

Then Elsie spoke up. "And how is Eddie Lassa doing?"

"He's still in surgery," the surgeon replied. "Are you family?"

"I'm the closest thing he has to a grandmother."

The surgeon studied Elsie's honest face and then said, "He suffered minor internal bleeding, but what's taking so much time is a badly crushed hip. They are putting pins in to hold it all together."

Then they all turned and walked to the elevator. Drained and exhausted, Trish wanted to get home and lie down on her bed and sleep, to blot out the accident she'd witnessed and the terrible thoughts she was thinking. *How could he have done this?*

        ▭

AT NEARLY FIVE O'CLOCK the next evening, Trish waited outside Grey's hospital room while he dressed in the fresh clothing she'd brought. She was here to drive him home to Elsie. Elsie had taken this latest shock very hard and was trembling too much to be able to walk.

And she didn't even know all the facts. Shirley had volunteered to come and sit with her until Trish brought Grey home. But Trish had something else on the agenda, featuring Grey and Eddie. She knew just what she had to do.

She'd gone into work today as usual. After the sheriff had returned from briefly questioning Noah and Grey, she and the sheriff had discussed the facts of last night's collision. Noah remembered everything about the night before clearly from the phone call to the collision. But Grey had awakened in the hospital, not recalling anything about last night.

In hours of discussion, Trish and Carter had exhausted all the possible angles as to who had been responsible for last night's accident. But the twine on Grey's foot, the blow to the back of his head, the alcohol on his clothing but not in his system led them to believe he was not driving the car. And Eddie with a whiskey bottle in his pocket and helmet on his head, jumping from the moving vehicle made Eddie look very suspicious. Together the evidence had told the tale that convinced them who was responsible. But was last night the first time Eddie had been involved in a hit-and-run? Could they now believe her aunt Harriet, who maintained she'd only done the first two hit-and-runs?

Trish and Carter had carefully crafted a strategy for Eddie and Grey this evening. They hoped to shock an admission of guilt from Eddie. Or goad a memory from Grey. Or both.

Now Grey joined her in the hallway outside his hospital room. She smiled at him, keeping her lips from trembling. She wanted to kiss and hold him close, but tonight she'd come also as a deputy. "All ready?"

He nodded as though moving his head hurt him.

"Why don't we stop by Eddie's room and say hi?" she asked innocently.

He nodded carefully once more.

"You still can't remember anything about last night?" she asked as they walked down the hall together. No one had told him all the details about the collision. He'd just been told that he'd had an accident driving home last night. She had to play her part for Grey's own good.

"No. I hate not being able to remember," Grey admitted. "It's just like...just like..."

Just like the last time, she finished the sentence silently. The unfairness of what had happened to the man she loved seven years ago and which had almost been repeated last night, made her determined to help the truth finally come out.

As they approached Eddie's room, Trish slowed her pace and then she paused outside the doorway.

The sheriff's voice came clearly out to them. "Eddie, you can't tell me it didn't happen. I repeat, Officer Franklin saw you jump from the passenger side of Elsie's Chrysler. That's why you were hit. Plus you were wearing a helmet so you wouldn't injure your head. Why did you jump from the car?"

"I'm going to sue that deputy for hitting me," Eddie said in a thin, reedy voice.

"That deputy found Grey Lawson's right foot tied to the accelerator. Now why would you tie Grey's foot to the accelerator and jump from the car?"

"You can't prove I tied his foot there," Eddie whined.

Trish was aware that she hadn't had to ask Grey to stop and listen. He had stopped on his own and was already listening. She clenched her fists.

Eddie went on. "That deputy is sweet on Grey. Maybe she did it so it wouldn't look like Grey had done it again."

"Done what again?"

"Drove drunk and caused another accident. Haven't you figured it out yet? Grey's been doing all these hit-and-runs."

Grey clutched her elbow then, squeezing hard.

She nodded and laid a restraining hand over his.

"Why would Grey Lawson do that?" Carter asked.

"Repeating his crime. You know people do that. They repeat their crimes."

"Sometimes that happens and I think this is not one of those times," Carter said. "In fact, I can think of only one reason for you to hit Grey over the head with your wrench—"

"I never—" Eddie objected.

Carter cut him off. "We found the wrench thrown on the front seat of your truck near the job Grey was finishing. It looks like Grey's hair and skin are still on it. A simple DNA test will prove that. And we've already lifted your prints from the wrench."

"I don't know what you're getting at," Eddie blustered weakly, "but I'm a sick man—"

"You are a guilty man," Carter replied. "You are the one who's done the last three hit-and-runs. Why? Was it to stir up Noah and the Vallieres against Grey so he would be forced to leave the area?"

"You can't prove that," Eddie said.

"I can prove that you must have hit Grey over the head with your wrench. I can prove that you called Noah and told him to drive down Cross-cut Road. I can prove that you jumped from the moving car where Grey's foot was tied to the accelerator. Do you think we're idiots?"

———

FURY FLOODED HOT AND overpowering through Grey. He strode into the room. He jerked back the white curtain that shielded Eddie and the sheriff from view. "I remember now." Even his words felt fiery hot as they flowed up through his mouth, searing his lips. "I remember everything. You came to the house where I was working. You told me your battery needed a jump. I bent over your engine and then it went dark."

Grey stared at the one person whom he'd believed was his friend for life. The lava of violence roiling inside him frightened him. He felt himself shaking with it. "Why did you do that, Eddie? Tell me why."

Tears began washing down Eddie's bruised face. "I didn't want to, man, but you came back. I couldn't stand having you around. It made it all come back. I'm hardly hanging on to my job at Ollie's and living in that basement room I rent. I know I couldn't make it anywhere else. I had to get you to leave."

"Why, Eddie?" Grey asked, his words so low in his throat that they pained him. "It doesn't make any sense. How could you do that to me?"

Eddie's face crumpled. "Don't ask me that. Please."

"I think I can give you a plausible motive. Grey," Carter said in his quiet but relentless voice, "you weren't the one driving that night seven years ago, the night Jake Franklin and Darleen Valliere were killed. I talked to the owner of Bugsy's today.

"I asked him to recall whatever he could of that night. When I asked him if he had any idea which of you was driving that night, he said it was funny because he thought Eddie was the one with the car keys that night. But he never said anything later because Grey admitted to being the one who had been driving. He thought you two had switched outside and Grey had driven. But you, Eddie, you were driving the car that killed Darleen and Jake, weren't you?"

Eddie wouldn't meet the sheriff's or Grey's eyes.

Shock nearly choked Grey. "That's the truth, isn't it, Eddie?" Grey demanded, molten tears smarting his eyes now. "I could never remember what happened and I just took your word for it. When I woke up—unable to remember anything—in the bed beside you in the hospital, you told me I had been driving. And I believed you. Because surely my best friend wouldn't lie to me about something like that, would he?"

Eddie's ugly sobs filled the room and the monitor he was hooked to began beeping. A nurse hurried in. "I must ask you to leave now." She gave the sheriff a sharp look. "You can wait and interrogate this man when he's stronger."

Inside Grey was rocked by a tumult of emotions, too many to sort out, to identify. *Eddie lied to me. My best friend lied. Let me go to prison for seven years for his crime.*

"I'm done," Carter said, his tone revealing his complete disgust with Eddie. He led Grey and Trish out into the hallway.

Carter made eye contact with Grey. "As soon as I get the specifics of this nailed down, I'll be notifying both the district and state's attorney that you were wrongfully convicted and incarcerated." Carter took Grey's arm in his hand. "I'm very sorry for all you've been through."

Grey couldn't make himself react. Eddie's betrayal had shaken him completely. He was lost. He'd been sold out seven years ago by his best friend.

———

TRISH TOOK GREY'S HAND and led him toward the entrance of the hospital. It had been a shock for Grey. She and Carter had known that it would be a shock, but they'd been hoping that hearing the sheriff question Eddie might trigger Grey to remember, at least, what had happened last night.

It had worked but now she faced a man who'd spent seven years in prison for a crime he hadn't committed. A crime his best friend had let him suffer for. She needed to help Grey through this.

Penny suddenly appeared at her side. "Oh, I'm glad I caught you. Trish, Noah coded and he's just been resuscitated. He's bad. I've called Andy, but one of my friends, another nurse, said she saw you here. Come with me." Penny held out her hand.

"I was just going to drive Grey—"

"Let Grey take your car home. Later, you can use my car to drive home. I'll catch a ride with someone else when my shift finishes. Come. Hurry."

Trish was torn. Grey did not look well. She didn't want him to leave until they'd had a chance to speak, to sort this all out. But Penny tugged at her arm. Over her shoulder, Trish said to Grey, "I'll catch up with you at Elsie's. Here are the keys to my SUV." She tossed them to him.

He caught them and left without saying a word to her, his face shuttered.

OUTSIDE, GREY GOT INTO Trish's red SUV. He felt as if he'd been standing on solid ground. Then in Eddie's room, a sudden earthquake had shaken him off his feet and had carried him off to unknown territory. He pressed both his hands flat against the seat and pushed down hard. Eddie had driven the car that night seven years ago. They'd both been thrown from the vehicle on the driver's side. So when Eddie had realized that Grey didn't remember the accident, he'd told him that Grey had been driving. *I thought he was my friend. My best friend.*

Everything that had happened over the last seven years had been based on a lie. Why? Why hadn't he known, guessed?

Disbelief suddenly mutated again into rage, bone-melting rage. Grey pounded the dashboard until his knuckles were raw and bloody. *God, how could You have let this happen? You let them lock me away for something I didn't do? I've carried all the guilt for seven years and I was innocent!*

Grey had finally driven away. Night had fallen, cold and clear. The complete opposite of the damp foggy night just two days ago that had changed everything. Forever. Grey hadn't been able to drive home to his aunt. The anger, the fury he felt over Eddie's betrayal mounted and mounted until he thought he might harm someone or himself. He wanted to rage, break things. He wanted to pound Eddie into the ground and then spit on his bleeding flesh. Grey's wrath hit him in swell after swell like a wild squall on Lake Superior and it was just as frightening.

So instead, he drove up and down the county roads, past the scene of the last accident and past the one from seven years ago. An unnatural restlessness gripped him. His skin even crawled with it. In fact, he wanted to shake off who he was and become someone else. Someone else that had not been betrayed by his best friend...by his God.

Grey knew that what he'd heard tonight from Eddie's own lips and the sheriff's was the truth. Extreme, appalling truth. There were no words to express the wrenching chaos of his deep, deep betrayal. *Why didn't God bring the truth to light sooner? Why did I have to suffer seven years of being locked in a cell, forced to bear the humiliation of losing everything that made me a man?*

He turned the SUV toward the hospital. The sudden urge to hit Eddie impelled him. He could feel Eddie's face crumpling, bleeding against his fists.

Then ahead, the vivid yellow and green neon lights of Bugsy's beckoned Grey. He pulled up and parked by the entrance. He sat behind the wheel, staring at the many neon beer signs. The door opened and the country-western classic, "Your Cheatin' Heart," blared into the cool night.

A thirst for a drink more overpowering than any he'd ever felt crashed over him in alternately hot and bitterly cold tidal waves. He got out, opened the door and walked into Bugsy's.

The music blared louder inside, but it was as if his entrance had struck everyone inside dumb and immobile. Every eye turned toward him and every voice died. The song on the jukebox ended and there was complete silence. He thought he could even hear the people around him breathing.

He knew practically every face staring back at him. One of the guys he'd played high school football with and whom he'd seen working at the hospital stood and pulled out his cell phone. The man, cell phone to his ear, walked outside. Great, call and tell everyone Grey Lawson is drinking again. Pulsing with belligerence, Grey stalked to the bar.

Lamar Valliere was standing there. Staring at Grey. "It's

true then, isn't it? Harriet called my dad this evening. You weren't driving the night my sister was killed. Eddie was."

So the gossips had put it all together before he'd even been privy to the truth. Grey shrugged. He didn't want to talk. He needed a drink. Now. He turned to the bartender. "Whiskey. Straight up."

Behind him, someone pushed back a chair. A light hand touched his shoulder. "Grey, you don't want to do this."

He turned to see a dark-haired girl he'd dated in high school, a niece of Shirley's.

"They'll send you back to prison," she said. "Don't."

Grey didn't even look at her. "A whiskey straight up," he repeated to the bartender. Then he said over his shoulder, "I'm going to be exonerated, haven't you heard?" His voice dripped sarcasm. "The sheriff feels really bad about everything." He looked back at the barman. "Where's that shot?"

Looking at Grey from under his bushy salt-and-pepper eyebrows, the man poured the shot and set it in front of Grey. He cleared his throat. "Lawson, I'm sorry I didn't speak up all those years ago. But I thought I was mis—"

Before Grey could reach out and grasp the drink, Lamar took the glass and tipped it to his lips. "Thanks. I usually drink beer but tonight whiskey is just what I want."

Grey curled his hands into fists. Games, Lamar wanted to play games. "Another one," he barked. He glared at Lamar. "Do that again and I'll put you on the floor."

Lamar sipped the whiskey and leaned on his arm. "Maybe, maybe not."

Another whiskey appeared on the bar. The dark-haired girl snatched it before Grey could. "Yes, thanks, Grey."

Grey glared at her. She smiled and walked back to her companion at the table. "*I am not*—" Grey hit each syllable hard "—*playing games*. I want that whiskey. Now."

The bartender studied him. There was a sudden scraping

of chairs and those nearest Grey rushed up to the bar and began ordering drinks. The bartender walked away from Grey and began pouring drinks for his other customers.

Grey hit the bar with his fist. "Get me that whiskey or—"

"Or what?" Trish's voice rang out clear and true over the babble of voices.

Instant silence.

Grey turned to face her, his back to the bar. She stood just inside the door. His mind couldn't take in her presence here. "What? Where did you come from?"

"I called her," the guy he'd played football with said from his seat near the window. "I work at the hospital and I know what went down there today. Between you and Eddie. So I called Penny at the hospital, knowing she'd know how to get hold of Trish. I'm not slow. Anyone seeing your face when you walked in would have known you needed—"

"Needed what?" Grey snarled.

"Needed me," Trish finished. "Do you think Winfield has been clueless to what's been going on between us?"

Grey did not want to talk about this. He didn't want to talk at all. He wanted to drink whiskey after whiskey until he passed out. He turned back toward the barkeep. "I want that whiskey now. Or I'm coming over the bar and getting it myself."

Trish came up beside him. "Pour me one, too."

Grey felt the sudden tensing of everyone around him. It was as if everyone in the room were holding a collective breath. He gripped the edge of the bar. "I've just about had it with this, Trish. I'm going to have a whiskey. In fact, I plan on having several."

"Fine," Trish cut in. "I'll join you. If drinking is a good idea for you, it's good for me. Pour us two whiskeys, barkeep."

The man studied her from under his eyebrows. He walked over and poured out two more shot glasses of the amber liquid.

"How much do I owe you?" Trish asked, reaching into her pocket.

"On the house," the barman said.

Trish lifted her glass to her lips.

"Better drink that slow," Lamar cautioned from her other side, "if you're not used to the stuff."

Trish nodded and tipped it to her lips.

Grey grabbed her wrist, stopping her, spilling the liquor. "Put that down."

Trish gazed at him. "If you're drinking, so am I."

He squeezed her wrist. She stared at him, daring him. Everyone was watching them. Grey felt a sudden release inside him. The tension wasn't gone, but it had loosened around his heart. "I'm not drinking." He released her wrist.

Trish lowered the glass back onto the bar. "I've changed my mind, barkeep."

"No problem." The man took back both glasses.

"Shall we go?" Trish asked as if everything were normal.

Grey wanted to go with her. But he still needed to fight with someone, vent his anger. "You go."

She smiled at him. "I'm only going when you go and I'm only going where you go."

She was doing it again. Being fearless. Totally unafraid. And here in public, where everyone could hear. "What am I going to do with you?"

"If I were thirty years younger, I'd kiss her," the barkeep said with a wink.

"Yeah," Lamar agreed. "Why don't you kiss her?"

Grey stared at her. "Why did it all happen? I gave away seven years of my life for what?"

Trish moved closer to him. "Maybe we should call it a severe mercy. Grey, you aren't the man you were seven years ago. You are the man now you were meant to be. I wouldn't love you if that weren't true. Where would you be now if Eddie hadn't lied?"

Her question aggravated him. He wanted to brush it aside like a meddlesome bee.

"Where would you be now if Eddie hadn't lied?" she repeated.

"That's supposed to make it all right," he snapped. "It doesn't."

"God doesn't make life easy for us." Trish looked him straight in the eye. "He doesn't care if we're happy here. He's concerned about molding us into the people He knows we can be. Sometimes His love hurts. But where were you headed seven years ago, Grey?"

"Well, it wasn't heaven," Lamar replied for Grey, who stood there with his lips pressed tightly together.

Grey wanted to slug Lamar. Instead he roared at Trish, "I don't care! I'm mad. Mad at Eddie. Mad at God. It wasn't fair. I paid the price for Eddie's crime."

"So now you know what Christ felt on the cross," Trish said. "God didn't let anything happen to you that wasn't done to Him first."

Her simple words pierced him, a thin skewer through the heart. She'd spoken the glistening truth. God knew just how he felt, standing here and now. He'd felt it, too. And worse. A fierce feeling, almost a physical heat, burned inside Grey. Then it was all gone. All the anger, the outrage, the unfairness had burned away. He felt cleansed, weakened.

It must have shown because Trish reached out and grasped his arms. "Come on. Let's go home. My dad's stable, out of danger for now. Elsie's worried about you. I've been driving around in Penny's car looking for you. I was only a couple of miles away when Penny called me and told me you were here. Come on."

He let her lead him through the silent witnesses and

through the door. Outside in the fresh cool air, she nestled close to him and he wrapped his arms around her. She was filling the open ache inside him. He leaned down and kissed her forehead. "I love you, Trish."

She grinned up at him by the light of the neon signs and the stars. "I know that." Then she raised up and kissed his lips.

He drew out the kiss, letting it flow through him, a healing, reviving warmth and comfort. "I'll never let you go."

"I'm not going anywhere you aren't," she whispered.

Chapter 14

After Grey followed Trish to the hospital to return Penny's car, he drove them through the sheltering darkness to Elsie's in Trish's car. Elsie's Chrysler had been totaled. Just like Grey's guilt and resentment.

He walked into his aunt's kitchen. She got up slowly because of her trembling but threw her plump arms around him. "It's all over," she said, weeping. "The truth has set you free. At last."

Shirley had hugged him, too, and then left with only a wave and a smile. Now, Grey sat at the table, sipping fresh-brewed coffee and holding Trish's small, soft hand. This kitchen had witnessed much sorrow and worry this fall. It deserved some happiness. As his nerves continued to ease, he wanted one more mystery to be solved. "Auntie, I've never asked you, but what happened to my parents?"

Elsie looked at him, obviously wondering whether or not to tell him at this vulnerable time.

"Tell me," he said. "I can handle it."

Elsie's round happy face fell. "I loved my sister Marjorie very much. But she was so much younger than I. We were

209

nearly fourteen years apart in age. I was more like a mother to her than a sister." Elsie sighed. "I watched helplessly as she married a man who wasn't worthy of her and watched her soothe that pain with alcohol. Then your dad ran off with some woman who was passing through town. It humiliated Marjorie. She took up with some guy that came up every year to fish. He asked her to go away with him."

Grey listened but the story almost didn't touch him. It was like listening to the story of some other person's life. Except that a few flashes from his childhood suddenly became clear. His mom crying inconsolably. His mom passed out on their couch. A guy he didn't like coming by their trailer, staying overnight.

"When she told me she was going, I insisted that she leave you with me. The guy, his name was Sheers, said it was a good idea. That they could make a fresh start, not take you away from the town you were used to till they were settled. I told her that she should give formal guardianship of you to me—just in case anything happened to her. I got the guardianship papers and she signed them." Elsie wiped her moist eyes. "After she left, she called once. But I never heard from her again."

"Why?" Trish whispered.

Elsie shrugged. "I think things must have gone bad with Sheers. Maybe. Anyway, Marjorie was drinking so much by then her health was suffering. I think it was easier just to let Grey stay with me."

Elsie patted his arm. "You were so angry with her when she left like that, I don't think she could face you. She knew she was doing wrong leaving you, but she didn't have much self-respect left by then. Don't judge her too harshly. She meant well. I think she actually thought she would come back for you. But she died within a short time. Sheers had already buried her by the time he sent me a two-sentence note letting me know. That's the last I ever heard from him."

Elsie sighed and slumped in her chair as if exhausted.

Trish rose. "Let's get Elsie to bed."

Soon, only Trish and Grey were awake. He sat down on the sofa in the small neat living room. She curled up beside him and laid her head on his shoulder. "Everything will be all right. No more worries."

He tucked her closer and kissed her silken hair, content just to hold her near him. "No more worries," he murmured against her soft cheek. *Thank you, Lord, for giving me this fearless woman.*

━━

FIVE DAYS LATER, TRISH walked into her father's hospital room. He'd been moved from ICU the day before. She leaned down and tried to kiss him.

He pulled his face away.

"Why do you do that?" she asked. "I'm your daughter. You've been very ill and I've come to see you. In this situation, a daughter kisses her father hello."

He twisted his face in a grimace. "What do you want?"

She sat down on the bedside chair. "I want to understand you."

He let out a sound of frustration, something like a growl.

"I know that losing my mother and your twin brother—"

"And the rest of my brothers and sisters," he added irritably. "Are we going to have a counseling session here?"

She sighed. "Father, I just want to love you."

"Of course you do. I'm your father. You should love me. Who took care of you after your mother died? Who made sure you had clothes to wear and food to eat? Do you think it was easy being mother and father to all of you? You haven't raised even one child, but you think you can tell me what I ought to do, what I ought to feel."

She rested against the back of the chair and thought over his words. "Everything you've just said is true," she said at last. "But my question is, why are you always so angry?"

"I'm not angry," he snapped. "I just don't have anything to be happy about. And you've been a pain in the neck this year. I told you I didn't need you to move back here and start taking care of me. I can still take care of myself."

"All right. I won't take...or try to take care of you anymore."

"Good," he snapped sourly.

"I suppose by now you've heard that Eddie Lassa is the one who is responsible for your brother's death?"

"Yeah, everyone in Winfield's been calling to tell me. And everyone thinks I should apologize to that Lawson."

Well, yes, that would be the normal reaction. But from Noah's harsh expression, hope for that didn't look promising.

Before she could reply to this, Grey walked in. He'd come with her, but had let her come in alone first. "I don't expect an apology, Mr. Franklin. I just hope you won't still hold me responsible for your brother's death."

"Even if you weren't driving the car that killed Jake," Noah growled, "you're still just as culpable as Eddie. Two people died that night and I won't forget your part in it."

"I'm sorry to hear you say that, sir," Grey said.

Trish rose and came to him, taking the hand he offered her. Grey continued, "Because, Mr. Franklin, I'm marrying your daughter as soon as possible. I wasted my twenties on alcohol and the last seven years in prison. I want to start our family right away and Trish agrees."

Noah glared at them. "If Trish marries you, I'll disown her."

"Sorry, Daddy," Trish spoke softly, "but you already did that when I went off to become a cop against your wishes, remember? And in reality, you put me out of your heart, two days after my ninth birthday, the day we lost Mom. I love you and I honor you as my father. But I'm not going to let your anger and spite keep me from the man I love." Moving close to Noah, she tried to kiss his forehead but he pulled away. She pursed her lips. "Daddy, Andy and Chaney will be in to visit later. Pete and Mick are on their way. Bye."

She let Grey walk her outside. He squeezed her hand and she looked up and smiled at him. "I love you, Grey."

"I love you, Trish."

And it was enough to rest in God's arms, to love and be loved.

———

THE PLEASANT AROMAS of another Sunday dinner eaten at Andy's lingered in the living room, adding to Grey's mellow state of mind. All of Trish's four brothers had come with wives or girlfriends and children, even Pete who lived out of town. Young Jake sat on Grey's lap, as if staking claim to him. The Packers game was on and the guys were all watching the game. The women were in the kitchen planning the small intimate wedding for the second weekend in December.

Chaney came over and nudged Young Jake to go and play Hungry Hungry Hippos with his cousins. When his son was out of earshot, Chaney leaned over and said, "I went to see Rae-Jean on my day off. She's decided to carry the baby to term."

Grey leaned closer to Chaney's ear. "Is she keeping the baby or putting it up for adoption?"

"She hasn't decided yet."

Grey nodded. "A difficult decision."

Chaney frowned. "I'm going to have a paternity test done after the baby's born. I told her if it's my child, we can discuss keeping it and I'll support the kid. But we're not saying anything to Young Jake till we know what we're doing."

"Wise."

Trish and the other female relatives filtered in. Trish pushed between Chaney and Grey, grinning. "It's all planned. Grey, all you need to do is get the license, buy a new suit and pay for the flowers."

"Yes, and my wedding gift," Elsie said, sitting down on an armchair brought into the room for her, "will be the deed to my house and all the land that goes with it. I assume that you and Trish will want to add on to my house. I'm expecting grandnieces and nephews." Elsie beamed.

Chaney stood up. "You see how it goes when you ask a woman to marry you? You'll be taking orders from her for the rest of your life. Be forewarned."

Grey chuckled. It felt good. He tugged Trish closer, her warmth flooding him with pleasure and joy. "What? Trish giving me orders? This sweet woman who's so quiet and shy? Telling me what to do?" Grey shook his head. "Chaney, you don't know what you're talking about." And then Grey laughed out loud.

The whole room erupted with laughter. And punching his arm, Trish was laughing the loudest.

Epilogue

On the Saturday before Thanksgiving, Sylvie Patterson sat in the front of the sunlit church glowing with a profusion of golden chrysanthemums. She was watching Audra and Carter say their wedding vows before Pastor Ray. As soon as they were finished, Shirley and Tom, who now stood up as matron of honor and best man, would switch roles and become the second bride and groom at this double wedding. Out in the pews sat Grey Lawson and Trish Franklin who would be married in three weeks. They were holding hands.

Sylvie gazed around the church. She was the only woman under thirty sitting alone. And she would only be twenty-nine for a few more months. Familiar feelings of being set apart flooded her. She tried to fight them, counting all the blessings she had, but the loneliness would never be banished.

The man forever associated with what set her apart sat on the other side of the church. He hadn't been seen here for years. What had brought Ridge Matthews back to Winfield?

DEAR READER,

I hope the story of Grey and Trish spoke to your heart. Surely Grey knew how Christ felt when he said to Judas Iscariot, "You betray me with a kiss." No one makes it through life without some betrayal at some time. And, of course, it's most painful when the source of that betrayal comes from those we never suspected, even from our "loved" ones. I hope that reading Grey's struggle will strengthen your faith that God does have a plan for each of our lives, and that even the most difficult situations can be for our own good. Trials come in various forms—illness, death, estrangement of a spouse or child. No one goes through life untouched by these. Turn all your troubles over to God. He is the great healer. May God bring you through as gold that has been through the fires of life. May God bless you in whatever circumstances you find yourself today.

THE NORTHERN SHORE series continues with the next book, FATAL WINTER.

A Carol Award–winning author delivers a page-turning work of romantic suspense! Bookstore owner Sylvie and detective Ridge share a painful history — but when they discover the dead body of Sylvie's cousin, they have no choice but to work together to unravel the truth...

What readers say:

"This book grabs your interest on page one and never lets up. Sylvie and Ridge and various family members are well developed and believable...This typical small town mystery is superb!"

"It was nonstop action from beginning to end and a great addition to the Northern Shore Intrigue series. Each book is a standalone with no cliffhanger...

She creates her characters with such detail you can almost

see them and the storylines draw you in as a participant. Twists and turn, love and mystery."

Winter Fury~ "There are layers of things going on. This book is well thought out and worth every moment of your time!"

Six books in this series:

Precarious Summer, Book 1

Bitter Autumn, Book 2

Fatal Winter, Book 3

Beneath Northern Lights, A Holiday Story, Book 4

Uncertain Spring, Book 5

Ominous Midsummer, Book 6

WITHDRAWN

9 798766 285656